More praise for *Diddy Wah Diddy: A Beale Street Suite*

❝ *Diddy-wah-Diddy* is an outlaw work, riffing
connections faster than the eye can follow
or the mind can see, a narrative shapeshifter
at work and play, coming off like some
literary Coltrane, dancing through waves
of cascading metaphors and narrative riffs,
voices and visions, startling conjunctions and
intuitive revelations. Literature doing what
it does best, forging a new way of seeing - a
profound meditation on the human condition
wrapped in a wild blue jazz solo. With *Diddy-
wah-Diddy*, Corey Mesler's unique voice
has found its fruition in a narrative tour de
force. Him and his work both stone cold
literary outlaws. Memphis on the cutting
edge. Representing."

—**Arthur Flowers**, author of *Another
Good Loving Blues* and *De Mojo Blues*

❝ They say--they used to say--that anything can
happen on Beale Street. Here it does."

—**Greil Marcus, author of** *Lipstick
Traces* and *Mystery Train: Images of
American in Rock and Roll Music*

" Corey Mesler writes riotous prose--fluid and lush and crazy. It's verbally rich and witty--half literary, half hoodoo. Imagine James Joyce on Beale Street with Elvis. Or something like that. Wacky but poignant!"

—**Bobbie Ann Mason**, author of *The Girl in the Blue Beret* and *Shiloh and Other Stories*

" With a playful, bebop narration, Corey Mesler transports the reader to the original Beale Street, where the heroes are musicians, bartenders, hustlers and strippers. Their dreams for a better life lead them to both love and betrayal, to angels and demons. And throughout, Mesler's prose gives the stories such a distinct rhythm—a sense of drumming, melody, and passion—that you literally hear the music."

—**Susan Henderson**, author of *Up from the Blue*

" The fevered dream of a Beale Street that could have been...or maybe was. Club BingoBango is the center of the known universe, with celebrities and local toughs and beautiful, dangerous women. Mesler has spun a tale of intrigue and delight."

—**Willie Bearden**, author of *Memphis Blues: Birthplace of a Tradition* and writer/director of the film, *One Came Home*

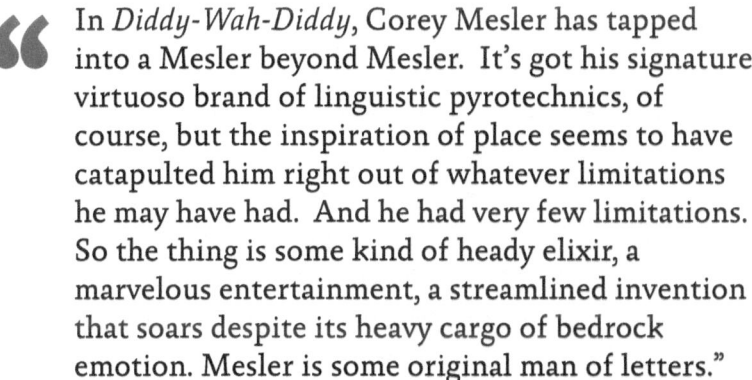

"Corey Mesler has cornered and captured the Memphis that has always interested me the most, the Memphis that's inextricably tangled up in its own mythology. And he's done it in such a way that we leave with the essential truth: Memphis is a phantasm, an accumulation of stories, most certainly a ghost town. As Michael Ondaatje gave us the New Orleans of Buddy Bolden, Mesler brings us to that other American city of song and throws us into its theater of strangeness, its lust and languor, its rage and bite. Not content to leave the mythic characters of Memphis under layers of sediment, Mesler brings them out, onto the streets, into the night again."

—**Warren Zanes**, author of *Dusty in Memphis*, and former Vice-President of the Rock and Roll Hall of Fame

"In *Diddy-Wah-Diddy*, Corey Mesler has tapped into a Mesler beyond Mesler. It's got his signature virtuoso brand of linguistic pyrotechnics, of course, but the inspiration of place seems to have catapulted him right out of whatever limitations he may have had. And he had very few limitations. So the thing is some kind of heady elixir, a marvelous entertainment, a streamlined invention that soars despite its heavy cargo of bedrock emotion. Mesler is some original man of letters."

—**Steve Stern**, author of *The Book of Mischief* and the Jewish Book Award winner for *The Wedding Jester*

Also by Corey Mesler

Poetry

For Toby, Everything for Toby (1997) Wing & The Wheel Press
Ten Poets (1999) editor, only Wing & The Wheel Press
Piecework (2000) Wing & The Wheel Press
Chin-Chin in Eden (2003) Still Waters Press
Dark on Purpose (2004) Little Poem Press
The Hole in Sleep (2006) Wood Works Press
The Agoraphobe's Pandiculations (2006) Little Poem Press
The Lita Conversation (2006) Southern Hum
The Chloe Poems (2007) Maverick Duck Press
Some Identity Problems (2007) Foothills Publishing
Pictures from Lang and Fellini (2007) Sheltering Pines Press
Grit (2008) Amsterdam Press
The Tense Past (2010) Flutter Press
Before the Great Troubling (2011) Unbound Content

Prose

Talk: A Novel in Dialogue (2002) Livingston Press
We Are Billion-Year-Old Carbon (2005) Livingston Press
Short Story and Other Short Stories (2006) Parallel Press
Following Richard Brautigan (chapbook) (2006) Plan B Press
Publisher (2007) Writers Write Journal Press
Listen: 29 Short Conversations (2009) Brown Paper Press
The Ballad of the Two Tom Mores (2010) Bronx River Press
Following Richard Brautigan (full-length novel) (2010) Livingston Press
Notes toward the Story and Other Stories (2011) Aqueous Books
I'll Give You Something to Cry About (2011) Queen's Ferry Press
Gardner Remembers (2011) Pocketful of Scoundrel Press

Diddy Wah Diddy:
A BEALE STREET SUITE

Corey Mesler

Ampersand Books

Florida

Ampersand Books St. Petersburg, FL www.ampersand-books.com

First Edition

ISBN: 978-0-9887328-5-8

Cover design by Matthew Revert and Pequod Book Design.
Interior by Raheel Ahmed

Illustrations by Amy Crook (www.antemortemarts.com).

· ·

Ampersand Books would like to thank Jennifer Rigsby, April Sopkin, Lindsey Silken, and especially Jessica Haeckel of Gemiinii Riisiing (www.gemiiniiriisiing.com)

· ·

S PECIAL T HANKS:

Sam Tickle, Rebecca Tickle, Jennifer Bridges, Carla Bauer

For Cheryl, Toby and Chloe
of course

and for Steve, Margaret and Arthur
who were there first

and, finally,
for Ernest Withers, whose eyes have seen

Everything in this book, including its truths, is a falsehood.

ACKNOWLEDGMENTS

"History" appeared originally in *Epiphany*.

"Arms Akimbo" appeared in *Menda City*.

"Jack Croswaith and the Devil" appeared in somewhat different form in *Crossroads*. It is based on an African-American folktale which appears in Zora Neale Hurston's *Mules and Men* as "How Jack Beat the Devil."

"Conjuration" won 2nd place in the Tennessee Writer's Alliance Short Fiction Contest 1997 and then later appeared in *Summerset Review*.

"Santa Claus and Sam the Bartender" appeared in *Southern Voices, Volume 5: Christmas Stories*.

"Huck and Hominy" were in *Arkansas Review*.

"Write Em Right" first appeared in *Eye-rhyme*.

"The Night Elvis Came to Beale Street" first appeared in *The Fifteen Project*.

"Seven Finger Tucker" & "Sweet Annie Divine" first appeared in *Strawberry Press*.

"Scuff Maladicta: A Ghost Story" appeared in Coyote Wild and in the Meadowhawk Press anthology *Touched by Wonder*.

"Butterfly McQueen's Oscar: A Lie" was in *Story South*

 *I'm here to tell you*
That something was wrong.
Lucille was there
But Beale Street was gone."

from "Power to the People"
Mudboy & the Neutrons

 *Diddy-wah-diddy: another suburb of Hell, built since
way before Hell wasn't no bigger than Baltimore.
The folks in Hell go there for a big time."*

—— HARLEM SLANG
(from The Library of America edition of
ZORA NEAL HURSTON'S
NOVEL AND STORIES)

INGREDIENTS

History: A History

And so we went down to the Club BingoBango on Beale--and this was O 1930something when Beale was Beale I think you know what I mean, and there were four of us, near as I can recollect; Beanie Sullivan, the Irish bootlegger, Red Rolly Kastlecream, baseball's first black shortstop I think he was, Sweet Annie Divine and myself.

There was news out on the street and the Club was the center of that news and well we were just as likely to be involved as not.

They had this new sax man there from Idaho name of Alexander Jimspake, no one has to tell you what he's done since, and he was setting up and the drinks were going around and the Club's ceiling which was cake frosting I'm pretty sure was dark and far away.

Well we thought we'd live forever that night.

And the jazz was just heating up and this new sax man was blowing a barrelfull and our table was sort of loud and the hub of the wheel of happening I might add and people were stopping by buying drinks and such and talking about the space program or some such.

Sweet Annie Divine just lolled her big head around and licked her fat red lips and opened her wide wide eyes wider and said--

I am the Duchess now and the old Duchess put out to pasture.

And we thought sure she was.

The next table had a fine tall white woman dancing on it with nary a care and underpants that said "The unexamined life is not worth living" written crack to crack in cool red thread and there was a big fat man sitting there name of Samuel Pepys who was tighter than Dick's hatband banging on the table with his hamsized fist like to shake that white woman off.

About midnight Sam the bartender--the original Sam the bartender and not the one from Monroeville, Alabama who came along much later--picked up his gavel and called out--

Order in the court. We're gonna line the republicans along the wall and shoot the sunsabitches.

Which we did.

Red Rolly kept drinking kerosene and lamb's milk and talking about the big leagues.

Twentythousand leagues, Beanie Sullivan said.

There was some Bible readings, some card throwings, hoodoo, one or two illicit passes of hands under the table clothes relieving the pressures of the times, Sweet Annie having the sweetest palm since high school for sure.

Big skinny ring-wearing joker came up to Beanie Sullivan saying--

You're a bootlegger I've seen you.

Beanie Sullivan betraying not a little worry sweating under his spit curls and deerstalker cap until the fellow shot out one long thin hand saying--

Name's Darby O'Gill an Irishman's brother and the second cousin to Michael Robartes himself by God.

So we relaxed and the drummer flammed like a butcher on horse and Jimspake wheedled out long liquid noseblows till the Duchess, the new Duchess, announced there was a party at the White House and the president and his first lady ever were inviting black folks up to just talk for a while about what he called the State of Things.

There was a guy there somebody from the Rainbow

Club I think who used to room with Caravaggio in college and
he told us some tales like to never forget about that scene and
its since unrecognized repercussions.

Club BingoBango known as the Best Bar on Beale and
a place where a man still tips his hat to a drag queen served up
all the right concoctions: Zombi killers, Fire on the Dick, Live
Long and Prosper, Cucumber Zingers, I Love the Catskills,
Red Fish Blue Fish, Poseidon's Clap, The First Crucifixion,
Sorcerer's Deodorant, and a thing made with kiwis and stump
water which was the house specialty and which no one had
dared to name.

We tried them all.

The Duchess when she had a snootful began to
palaver about how she once slept with Freud while she was
vacationing in Antibes and how he was a member in good
standing yessir and we had to shut her up with some barbq
Sam kept around for just such occasions.

I remember no one like the Logical Positivists at this
time and much ballyhoo was raised about this with finger
wagglings and fist shakings and it I guess was pretty much
good natured for such a tempestuous bunch.

No one's gonna have Immanuel Kant to kick around
anymore, I remember saying.

Wildeyed cat came in shooting his pistol up into the
air bringing down ladlesful of icing and stinking the place up
with blue smoke hollering--

Names Robert Ford and I ain't no coward.

Huck, the bouncer, chastised him with a Louisville
slugger. It was that kind of night.

Somebody in the corner was singing offkey in a
cracked Mississippi accent--

> I gots four ugly women
>
> Giving me fits
>
> I gots two ugly sisters
>
> With sco-li-o-sis

--till the ivory man walked over slowly and catheterized him
into sadeyed silence.

Heard Lady sing that oncet. Can't stand to hear it since, Bones said.

About dawn the four of us--and a fifth, Ginger "Styx" Quetzlcoatl, drummer for the BamBam Five--stumbled out into the street where we headed up toward the river reflecting the first Tang-colored raze of sunrise and we ran into Allen Ginsberg and a friend of his he called Gabriel and a dog walked on two legs.

We invited them all along.

We started out for Arkansas or the White House or the Promised Land which might have been just another club I can't remember and Gabriel said he wanted to play us a little something and we said Fine fine...

Anyway that was around the time this cat called Albert Einstein spilled to me about this atom he was splitting which I started to tell you.

AC2013

Arms Akimbo: A Gest

> **"** I told a white fella once, I said, 'Hey man, if you were
> black for one Saturday night and on Beale Street,
> never would you want to be white again."
>
> Rufus Thomas

It was Arms Akimbo, the stripper, and the evidence she
manufactured, the letter she wrote which presaged neither
ghost avoidance nor shrinking by lightning, ran like this:

Dear .... ,

If you think I'll wait for you bacon'n'eggs, you've got
another thing coming. You done run off for the last time.
And etc.

anabellee yrs,

Arms

Life being life it was all out on the street and the few messengers who arrived arrived with one note of alarm in their otherwise unremarkable leaks and we killed those who made us sad and those who did not stuck around like yesterday's high-pressure system and became generally part of the action.

This was the city and the city had a million innocences but it had a million cankers also and this is the story of a couple of each and the people responsible and the people hurt but the consequences are left to historians. We loved and lost and loved again. I in particular though I want no part in the narrative other than voice. It was Arms' legend then and it's Arms' now. She was everything to everybody and even Styx could not believe in her for more than a night at a time though it was Styx who catalyzed and Styx who spoke the truest line about Arms which went like this and I record it here faithfully:

Arms was Arms and love is a bad face mask but a good remedy.

Styx Quetzalcoatl was most famously the drummer for The BamBam Five but at the time of this saga the Five were no more having gone the way of all flash and Styx was gigging at Ruby's four nights a week with an experimental fusion trio with Henry the Hammer Jensen on bones and a chick they called HoneyDo blowing any number of wild wind instruments. They were hot like most of the nights on Beale and a godly crowd nominally attended.

It was on one particular steamy night when the sidewalk was a stroll through a barbecue pit and the denizens were halfnaked and the other half unclothed that Arms wandered into Ruby's after her night's performance a few doors down at The Tainted Lady. Now it would be asinine to imply that Arms didn't know Styx already at least by reputation or Styx Arms since Arms was the most popular act on Beale what with the stoat and all but their paths had not necessarily intertwined if you see what I mean until this fated evening in midsummer broil.

Arms slid into the club like a trickle of semen and the music seemed to increase in syncopation and size and Styx certainly seemed to flail with renewed vigor though he himself might not have glommed onto why right at the outset. Arms insinuated herself into the ripening atmosphere and sat at a back table with Jimmy the Snake and one or two of the Tiller boys and the heat in the joint rose accordingly.

And on a break which shall go down in infamy Styx sidled over to the aforementioned way station in the dark desert of Ruby's All Night and Into the P Wee Hours Supper Club and Dance Hall and put a calloused hand onto the cheapsuited shoulder of Jimmy the Snake and said Howdo and nodded at one or two of the Tiller boys and smoked a look at Arms and said:

We met?

And Arms by way of howdo said in a dusky Ladyday kind of vocalizing:

We ain't but we gonna.

And I believe it was that night but of course how could I know being at least a third party that Styx and Arms consummated in the upstairs room of Oswald's boarding house where Styx hung his head and where the bed music carried down the stairs and out into the street where the ungloaming was tangerine and woodsmoke and it mixed with the still lively though muted sounds of some club band and the birdsong and cicadas from down by the river and day broke and it broke again and it was a new morning in Memphis and elsewhere.

Unbeknownst to our hero there was a spare wheel on this bike and it was the sort of a sticky wicket Styx was peculiarly sensitive about having lost one or two loves of his life to slicker men with slicker pitches and having walked away with a simulacrum of pride not showing nowhere but moreover with his tail tucked where the sun don't shine

especially on a black man. This certain third stone from the
sun was a gangster if that's not putting too fine a point on
it who was in and out of every club on Beale with his scaly
hands in many a pie, yes and we already passed his cohorts by
briefly earlier at the table at Ruby's and they were already as
this story staggers forward running off to tell the man himself
what transpired in the heat of the night at the table at Ruby's.
Though what they seen was hardly remarkable and what they
knew nugatory.

His name being Ricky the Rake Romito.

But backup to an earlier time at the gentleman's club
where Arms dances nights and meet a fellow exotic dancer of
Arms' who went by the honeyed moniker of Callie Pidgeon
and it was her overheated heart that Ricky first stole though
after he owned it like many of us have experienced it lost its
luster and lust and Ricky was trying to fling it from hisself
with the same determination he might put into a thumbscrew
or sidebet.

Now Callie was a white woman (with eyes the color
of nickels) and Ricky was as black as his heart and Styx was
the color of fine mahogany and Arms, well, Arms was sort of a
mochafied flypaper ginger (and when she stripped it was like
a long cool quaffa ice coffee like something under the skin
sexual and then again not just) and the only reason I mention
this is for the historical ramifications, better to be upfront
about, and though Beale had its magic which precluded
judgmentalisms there was and still is alive in the land a
smallmindedness which makes these distinctions requisite.
But let us saunter on.

Ricky and Callie went hot as Memphis in June
for a while but then like I say Rick went north and Callie
began to sense His Holiness not quite around much and she
confronted him in the club one night as she worked down
to just a G-string and kneepads and he seated himself in the
front down along the runway and soon as he was down Callie
noticed a small Puerto Rican girl about the size of a country

ham on his right arm and she went threeways berserk. She
leapt offa that runway limbs windmilling and Ricky lost a
cap off one of his front teeth and this little gal with him lost
her wig which went flying heavenward and set itself right on
Mona Jewel Mobly, the stripping comedienne, and things was
real interesting for about ten minutes or so. Until Ricky let
go a right cross which set Callie like a grounded jet back up on
that runway with her legs splitwise from her perfect rumpal
area and her breasts looking like prayers to the gods and her
eyes as crossed as Jesus.

And that was the end of Callie/Ricky and Ricky
shortly thereafter started in to messing with Arms and Arms
was all lonely and funky at this time and fell for his crooked
charm and she and Callie got real cool for a fortnight or so but
then they became best friends and told each other their hearts'
deepest recipes. And the deepest one was that now Arms had
awoken and she couldn't stand Ricky but she was deadon
scared of him and he was bound and determined she was his
until the atom split. And though this was an old story it was
as true as the dawn and Arms found herself a bird in a gilded
cage so to speak and Ricky used her like a flashy ring and here
about now enters our hero as you mighta guessed.

So Styx set about a courtship which is famous for its
intensity as well as its smoking intrepidness. Mostly he wrote
like he had never written before because he had never written
before, love letters leaking from him like seepage from a
wound and it was a wound, heartdeep and as serious as war.
Arms found letters in her mailbox, on her nightstand, tucked
into her panties lying light and hesitant in her drawers, tied to
the collar of wandering dogs. Notes drifted into her windows
at all hours; they arrived wrapped around rocks, bobbing into
her toiletbowl delivered by ball-cock floatation. They ran on
and on. They ran like this:

I love you more than either
of my hands, more than
my ball and chain.

I have half a hundred
amusing things to tell you, the
rain is electric, etc.
If you move away I will
change poles.
I would do anything for you,
silence, drugs, pillage, socialism.
I only want you out in the light
honey, I break jaws
for the Philharmonic.
Wake up the sorority,
I want to soliloquize.
Your eyes, where are you,
your eyes are after me.
What can I do, tear out
this sadsack blood sac, poke
out my blinkers.
I'll cut my teeth for you,
take a fancy sobriquet,
what, what?
Nothing is more noxious than
this, I cannot distinguish
this sodapop leakage.
I am mysterious to the point of
soap opera. The case is
this, what I want and all
is you.
excess and ohs,
Styx
Or:

Something I need is
festering like soup.
You are such a bright crow,
such an armload of lightning.
Or:

The love I have for you burgeons
forth like inflammation,
the love of art for the big
City, the love of a hunchback
for her little goat.

It was as relentless as weather, as seductive as eating.
Arms fell hard, believed in love, in its necromantic mystery, in
its pure power to transform. She was transformed.

They were a couple; coalesced. They were alive,
snapping their fingers to no particular rhythm, almost
vaporized with the tension between flying and just staying
themselves, yes. The destitute places in each of them re-lit.

They heard the same note all night. They dreamed
about a stationwagon, abandoned in a parking lot, on the
front seat four Polaroids of newborn babies. And, later,
about men standing at every door in a neighborhood, waiting
to knock, in every hand a freshly minted death certificate.
They awoke from their dreams and held each other, and the
dreams blew away and at dawn, always, they made love with a
thoroughness nearly previously unknown in this old world.

"Nothing is written."

Lawrence (you know, of Arabia)

This is what Styx had written on the tailend of one of
his many love letters, as cryptic as a prophecy. Arms didn't
know whether this freed her or imprisoned her and she didn't
rightly care at the moment. At the moment.

What was Mr. Big doing while this was transpiring, where was Ricky? From most accounts we get the idea he was in St. Looie on business, the devil's business I'm saying, and this is what we should call the official version, though it is my personal conviction that he was elsewhere. Now I don't know where your religion takes you and I ain't gonna talk about mine none either but I believe as sure as I'm the nameless narrator of this narration that Ricky wasn't around while Arms and Styx were wrestling with the capital L because he had transformed himself into an animal spirit and he was prowling around the river bottoms of Northeastern Mississippi as he was wont to do occasionally to re-fill his empty metaphysical tank. I'm just saying.

Ricky was a werewolf, there it is.

So he didn't come into the city for awhile.

Immediately:

Arms in Styx's arms.

Styx working his left hand along the fallow river bottoms of his paramour's lower back, Arms pushing her furry pubis bone hard against her man's hip.

Styx all mouth on Arms' bare midsection, tongue here and there, naval basing; Arms' long ladyfingers juggling two balls at once, keeping Styx in the air.

Styx running one definite if not definitive drummer's finger down the crack in the world, finding the source of warmth and moisture, Arms panting moving like an immaculate creation seeking the always difficult not to say hard center of things.

Styx and Arms akimbo, a Catherine Wheel, heads in each other's townsquare, devoted moles, Arms' mouth full, Styx soliciting.

Arms on Styx, Styx on Arms, Styxarms, Armstyx, rocking, rocking, and then one long low saxophone note, the one pure note, the fix, the cure, the sound of the world being torn apart and born again.

And in this oblivion they did not hear, children, the return of the man who could become lupine. They were not aware that danger was near, no. Across town, in an office building on North Main, in one of those urban-renewal catacombs of soullessness and progress where the spirits of the dead among the living are sanitized and made presentable, Ricky the Rake threw down his bag, threw up his lunch (the fetlock of a Wolf River Wild Pig) and put his ear to the wind. He stepped out onto the balcony and lifted his head to the southwest and a foreshortened howl slipped into the breeze off the river, fluttered toward town, toward the east end of Beale Street where Styx and Arms were falling back limp as sacks into the world of men.

I don't know where you hail from stranger but on Beale Street news travels fast, so fast it is breathed in and out with the greasy odor of barbecue, and Ricky was not in the fungal backroom of The Tainted Lady five minutes before Jimmy the Snake so named for obvious reasonings was forking tongue into his ear with bad news, horrible news, news no man should reckon with without reckoning with it.

Now Ricky was cool, he was cool. He stapled Jimmy's paisley tie to Jimmy's pustuled forehead, pulled his pants down and threw him into the middle of Second Street, took a deep breath and called the Tiller boys to his office at the club (one of many he had at various and diverse clubs on Beale).

"Bring me that drummer," he seethed through verdant teeth.

When half a beat later they threw before him a peddler of women's toiletries they had found trying to interest the hookers in depilatory cream Ricky sat the Tiller boys down for a long talk during which they seemed to glom onto the situation at hand and set off anew in pursuit of their quarry.

Styx was helping Arms glue flowers onto the ample rump of their dear companion Callie with a homemade potion of flour salt and sperm designed to stick quick but still release quicker than the jism (Styx' mental and physical contribution to their agglutinative endeavor) which earlier that afternoon both women had helped him donate to the cause, taking turns with various body parts separating Styx from his precious elixir. This all in the spirit of close comradeship you understand as the girls harbored no lingering jealousies and often Styx helped them with their respective acts, yes, with primed heterosexual responses to this bump or that grind and rewarded them especially with the glory of his fullsized erection when something was sure as fire first rate.

What he was doing now.

"Right here on your perfect lower left cheek a perfect hibiscus, dear one," Styx said as he took a little longer than was necessary to paste it in place.

"Styx you old hounddog," Callie said with a tinkle. "Hadn't you done worn out today that maleness you carry around?"

"Never child," Arms answered and put her tongue into Styx' inner cheek as she remunerated him with a wet one.

"This is not exactly FT-deum," Styx said, running his hand through a curve of poppies.

When Callie's tailgate looked like a nosegay from Victoria's most secret secret, the three sat down to a quick repast of lemonade with quinine, eggrolls and avocado slices. Arms was just licking her fingers to prepare a speech when the door burst inwards in resplendent gangster movie fashion and Arms' speech went the way of the ending to *The Castle*.

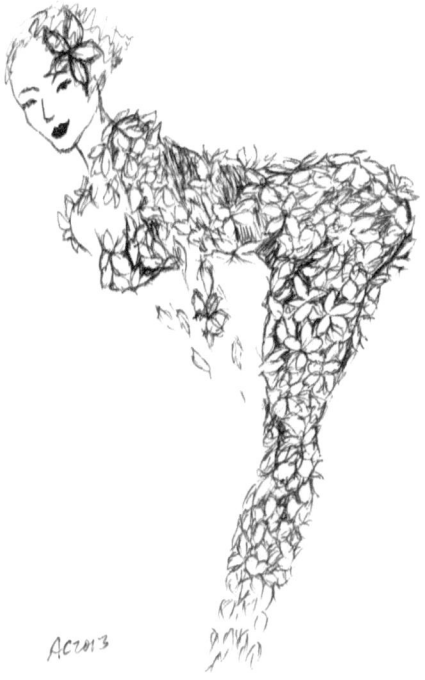

"Grr," the Tiller boys said, practically in unison.

"Boys," Styx said.

The Tillers tilted this way and that bumping into costume racks and cardboard boxes in their foray across the room not forgetting to gaze longingly at Callie's near denuded form partially obscured with bouquets. Was that a nipple or a pistil, pubic hair or pedicel cilia?

They finally made it to Styx's side and each took a meaty musician's bicep roughly in their sweaty rookers.

They requested that he accompany them.

Ricky was spitting chicken wing bones into a metal trash can with musical aplomb, a rhythm Styx who was never tuned out tuned into, when Styx who was not a brave man by any stretch strode toward him spats splayed pugnaciously.

"Man about town, man of the world, johnny on the spot, man of the hour," Ricky said in greeting.

"Long may you run," Styx approximated back.

"As I live and breathe," Ricky said.

"Speak to me of many things."

"Can't buy me love," Ricky ricocheted.

"As my mama used to say philosophically, Kant never did nothing," Styx replied, relaxing into the stream.

"You're an ex-drummer," Ricky off-handed.

"And you're a werewolf," Styx answered, turning on his sharp heels and moving out the door, out onto the street and out of sight. The next time we hear from him it will be under different circumstances indeed.

Ricky was all rage and grief and he overflowed like a sputtering kettle spewing henchmen into the hemisphere with sharpened intentions and a halfcocked ideation of semidestruction and mayhem, all with Styx's name on it. Styx, we don't know how, it's missing from the legend, was temporarily disappeared.

With this Ricky was satisfied and was soon enough at Arms' door with goldtoothed smiles and bouquets of violets (which only an hour before he had peeled off the tempestuous backside of Callie Pidgeon after burying his face in her fields which served to mollify an angry but lonely Callie who succumbed to Ricky's backhanded charms against her better judgment and allowed him to snake his way between her blackeyed Susans and moisten the warm loam of her innerness, as Ricky, free from the noisome interference of that bat-legged drummer, attempted to re-establish his proper place in both women's lives {feeling as he did that suddenly he could tame any filly, a potent, though potentially foolish, surge of manly power, linking him, in his delusion, to all womankind} using necromancy and wolfish allure). Arms let him in, awash in worry and lachrymose despair as Styx had been gone now for two weeks. Ricky was a rickety comfort; Arms leaned on him gingerly, as one would a tower of Tinkertoys, moldy Tinkertoys. When Ricky patted her pleasant shoulder and asked if there was anything he could do, Arms' warning system knocked out in the storm, she blubbered and fizzed into his embrace. Ricky slipped a sweaty palm under Arms' arm, his goal the tender, beating swell of the side of her right breast, and Arms was off the couch and on the floor, howling to be left alone, completely alone.

Alone Arms began to imagine that Styx had been a phantom, an ensorcellment of neediness and wishful thinking, a spook born of emptiness and longing and that their cohesion had been an illusion. This is a dangerous time and you all know who've been there that the soul is a jerry-built engine and requires constant lubrication and sometimes cheap store brands look as good as a sweet dose of 10W-30.

Arms doubted.

Arms stewed.

Arms darkly dreamed, a specter of aloneness.

She thought maybe Styx was a phantasm, a spook that sat by the door and now, as is only right, he had gone out that door.

(Actually, a solid though frightened Styx had been taken, Tillerwise, to the Gulfa Mexico and put into a rowboat bout the size of an owl and a pussycat and pushed toward Cuba or Haiti or points southward. The Tillers considered this a job well done and went home, whistling. Styx drifted adrift for days living on gullspit and fishblood, only to surface, drylanded if not drydocked, later in the story.)

She and Callie got together for tea and sympathy
and together worked on re-sexing their respective routines,
bringing in kitchen implements, bathtoys, pictures of
ex-presidents, baby blankets, to spice up their, wrongly
perceived, fading strip careers. Together they perceived
that things were better, that their individual appeals were
not gone but stronger (hips as round as the Earth's rotation,
breasts like the faces of gods) and they rightly praised each
other's lubriciousness, and knew that, though they could
fall into each other's laps and temporarily dispel that well
of loneliness, that they would still need a gender-different
opinion.

Off the street came simple Freeman Blemish,
downtown's sweet and flatulent ragman, all smiles and watery
eyes, unsure of his ability to serve as judge in what he did not
understand was a display of an age-old resplendence. And
when Arms and Callie, in tandem, worked their disrobing
witchcraft, Freeman spittled and wept and farted, the
end result of which was a puddle of ragman, a worthless
adjudication, to be sure.

And this is how Ricky the Rake worked his way back
into the two women's good graces, presenting hisself as
connoisseur extraordinaire, as The Final Word in taste and
appreciation. As Mr. Testosterone. The women would strip,
and Ricky would rate. This is how it was. At least in this
tangled old tale which is a pulse-rate off tangentially from an
accurate rendering of tired reality.

Nightly, or more correctly afternoonly, the strippers
and The Boss met for tuning up, for a little sexual threesquare,
and every evening the girls had a new wrinkle to their acts,
and though age was a constant moss on their clappers, they
began to ring as clear as any twenty-year-old belles on Beale or
beyond, yes sir, and when word got around that there was two
strippers at The Tainted Lady could turn you inside out with
desire, that club became the hottest spot this side of the sun,
man, and those two beautiful women the toasts of that sunny

Dixie town. So, afternoons were for practice: Showtime sometime being *ménage* time (Ricky partial to a particular kind of oralism and analism which his wolfish side relished and which required two females and two sets of lubricated orifices) and nighttimes reserved for The Show of Shows. Seven nights a week. Yearround. Wearing thin quickly, our two stars, tarnished by fatigue and utilitarianism, cottoning on to Ricky's devilishness once and again and that fading spark of wishing left in Arm's soul for her departed Styx began to grow like Tinkerbell's light, a small tintinnabulation becoming brass cymbals, a symphony in her soul. Arms missed her man.

And soon the threesome, tiresome, became a twosome, Ricky's true attentions obviating. He gravitated toward his goal, and Callie, spurned again, grew morose to the point of old age and began to bend and wither, curling like an ash, dissipating. Callie's light began to dim.

Three weeks passed. Ricky and Arms were fucking regularly, void of any feeling, dogbushed, a wolf and its prey, Arms so empty she was listless: she was without list.

Arms floundering in the fantods.

And at the club, as her act grew in strength and popularity, she found herself (after losing herself so to speak) the sole act, Callie having inconveniently dematerialized. Arms still stripped like a turpentine whirlwind, clothes evaporating from her seemingly flying to the winds, sucked off by natural forces, and she spun and spun, as if subject to that same willful wind, an abandoned dreidel, denuded like a winter tree, while the legions cheered. Arms naked was still, let's say it one more time, worth the price of ammunition.

One night, Arms luded into nodding dollhood, on Ricky's overly hirsute elbow, the two misfits drifted into Ruby's looking for a little busman's holy day, a drink without their fingerprints already on the glass--Live Long and Prosper, Ricky's libation of choice, Arms sticking to straight Stoli on top of her medicine. Some goldtoothed clan pulled the man aside and left a limpnecked Arms at the bar humming "Mississippi Lowdown Blues" to herself and staring at the profile of the old crone next to her without seeing and the old crone oblivion bound as well.

A light from the attic cracked the code of the two individuals' stupor and eye to eye they stared until dawning came slowly on little cat's feet. It was Callie Arms was settled next to: Callie like maybe she'd look in the next millennium. Callie sucked dry and spindled, an apple-core face, limbs like twisted rope, hair of steel wool: Callie, gone over to the other side and still walking round.

"Calgal!"

"Oh, Arms!"

"Lawsy, Lawsy, what in the world? What in the fucking world?"

"Arms, Arms," Callie bawling now.

"Speak to me, gal."

"Arms."

"Cal, I'm gonna slap the shite outa you."

"I'm under a spell, Arms. I'm under a mutha of a spell. It was Ricky did it, it was him. Oh, Arms," and she broke down into mumbly sobs.

"We gonna take care of this, Calgal. You listening to me? We gonna see to this."

And Arms was off that stool and striding out the door when Ricky caught her from behind. Some say it was a sap Arms swung like a Louisville slugger, some say a sock full of fishing weights, some say it was just her sweet balled up fist, but something powerful caught Ricky the Rake upside his jaw and landed him on his goldwatch, out like a waterless gar on the sawdusted floor of Ruby's, out like a mothergrabbing light. Something powerful caught Ricky and set up the penultimatum of our plot, you see, getting us from there to where we going.

It was magic commencing.

Some say.

As storytellers tell: Meanwhile. In the Crescent City way down south where the humidness is thick as stupor and mosquitoes sound like bandsaws and the music is a sometimes dreadful sometimes soulful mix of gumbo and blues and marching bands on a street off a street around Tchoupitoulas south of Calhoun in a backdoor alleyway stood a man who was all man and all something else.

He was all man and he was the devil.

He was darkeyed and beetlebrowed and sweat ran off him like frog secretions and he stared out into the darkness like he own the darkness and he whistled low between his teeth.

He whistled like he was calling something unearthly and expected it to come.

Without going any further lemme tell you that this partman was formerly a drummer in Memphistown, formerly with the BamBam Five, formerly the lovemate of our own Arms Akimbo, and he was formerly called Mr. Quetzelcoatl by many and Styx by them what knew him best. And Styx, though crossedover, he was still but Quetzelcoatl he was no more, now nomenclatured surwise Ygg.

And no one knows from whence that name came and no one asked.

Styx spat once, glanced at the moon (and the moon glanced back), turned and went in. He bent to pick up a beatup portmanteau and he stood for a moment in that dingy frontroom gathering his thoughts.

He stuck his head into the doorway of the adjoining room and spoke low like his voice came from elsewhere besides his throat.

"I'm leaving," he said.

And out of the dim a voice answered. It was the voice of the dim, a woman's voice.

"It's time."

"Yes."

"You ready."

"If that's a question, yes."

"You is."

"I'm owing you."

"Time'll take care a that. You be on that train."

"Am I—?"

"Yes."

"Sure."

"Only alone can you be sure."

"Your strength, its—"

"Old as Scratch."

"Yes."

"Go on now."

"All right."

And with that he turned and the night surrounded him, a black vaginal night. He slunk back toward Memphis like a viper, like a hellhound.

Back in Memphis beside the roiling uncoiling brown snake of the Mississippi on the street of life on the street of the blues in the middle of an otherwise insensible afternoon in the back room of a nondescript boardinghouse near the Malco theatre where the movie was some new talkie starring men and women who were living out everyone's dreams drinking and fucking and snorting and being paid the ransom of kings but who projected through the projector a dazzlingly torpid sense of excitement and simultaneous wellbeing that the rubes lined up they lined up they all lined up there was a confab commencing. Arms and Callie, Callie and Arms.

Heads together like witches, eyes rolling inward. They were intent on breaking the spell of the wolf, for spell it was. Mesmer magnetism.

"We need to put him down like an old dog, dogbody him, put him down hard."

"With no evidence."

"No body."

"No corpus yes."

"Let the river take him."

"Too risky."

"Feed him to the hounddogs."

"They won't eat one of their own."

"Burn him."

"He won't burn."

"Chop him up, pieces too small to bother with, scatter him down Highway 61."

"Too messy."

"What then? What then?"

"We need magic."

"Selma."

There lived near Beale in those days a very old woman, some say a conjurewoman, an aeromancer, and her name was Selma. Legends abound about Selma, conflicting yarns, some reverent about her powers, most descrying a fraud.

She knew the mojo, the conqueroo, spake to the spirits, sure. But agreement was she used it to scare kids, fleece the fleeceable. No serious magic there and besides she was old, old as the delta.

Her house, round by Central High School, was so off the street, one thought one had found an empty lot, a derelict address. Selma's place sat behind a doctor's house, a respectable, upright white man who had a daughter at Miss Hutchison's, a son at Yale. Selma had something on the good doctor, it's told, something from wayback, when the whiteheaded whiteman was a college man, looking for love. It's told they had a child together, this once wild whiteman and this black witch from East of Eden, but this is fabulous, this is taletelling. To travel to Selma's through the doctor's backyard was like parting a curtain on the good, solid world. Like entering another element, maybe air, maybe something else.

Arms and Callie knew the way to Selma's.

The three women met in the sitting room, on dusty Victorian furniture, over dusty madeleines.

"It's a man, ain't it?" Selma broke the stillness.

"Yes'm," Callie, who looked as old as Selma, spoke quickly.

Selma picked up a memory cookie and found the

middle distance. "I had a man once, oh once," she said, and maybe she was casting back to a secret assignation in the garage of a young med student, whose uncircumcised love would know her and, because it had to, move on.

"He's made Callie age," Arms put in.

"Hmmm," Selma said, studying Callie like she was in a cage. "No one can make a person age. Come from within."

"He done it," Callie said, a might shakily.

"Can't undo that," Selma said and nodded her head, agreeing with herself.

"We want him rearranged," Arms told Selma a tad defiantly.

"That I can do," she said, and after a long pause, a long blank space in the world, Selma cackled a bloodchilling cackle.

And when the women left they were not confident, carrying their little asafetida bag of wrinkled herbs. They looked at each other and managed weak smiles: they were heading toward hell armed with a tumbler of tepid water.

The Tiller boys were in bed with twins (yes, the famous fanfoot Schweik twins, the fanfeet if you will, Isabela and Adelaide, who stripped for heads of state worldwide and then went on to profitable careers as literary agents), in twin beds, side by side in the overly large foyer of Ricky Romito's lofty warehouse apartment. They acknowledged the entrance of Arms and the old crone by her side only with sideglanced nods, concentrating as they were on the four bouncing breasts alive above them.

"Oh," one Tiller said.

"Uhh," the other one said, seemingly to Arms.

The women breezed by them, determination in their darting eyes.

Ricky was at his desk when the pair burst in, head back, asleep perhaps, or daydreaming, the avengers thought. Actually Ricky was getting sucked off by a new waitress he'd hired, a teenager from Central, who smacked her head on the underside of the large desk under which she was concealed.

"Ow," she said, rising into view, a sad smile as she lazily covered her small pink breasts. She had an ebony optic, a fresh percutaneous puncture on her snake-thin arm.

"What the fuck?" Ricky roared.

"Jigsup," Arms said, her voice as shaky as the cheerleader's knees as she shuffled into her clothes.

"Scram," Ricky said to his new employee, and she did.

"Bye," she said running on tiptoe past. "Oops," they heard her say in perfect Doppler, as she whisked through the foyer.

Ricky's face began to lose its apoplexy and he settled back into his overstuffed chair.

"C'mere, Arms, and finish this job," he grinned.

Arms slipped a finger through the tiestring on her bag of tricks. She stared into the red eyes of her nemesis.

"And you, old woman, make tracks. Arms and I have some business to attend to, I'm thinking of making her a partner in the club."

Ricky detumesced, losing interest in that side of things temporarily.

Arms reached into the bag and held out what looked like a small quantity of tobacco. Ricky looked at it. Callie looked at it.

Ricky reached over and plucked it from Arm's palm and tossed it between cheek and gum.

Callie and Arms said a short incantation which they had not practiced and sounded in unison more like a rumble of dyspepsia. The three stared at each other for a few heartbeats.

"Well," Ricky said. "What else?"

The women didn't know what else. They were without voice. They seein' a wolf.

And as sudden as cloudcover Ricky's face contorted, twisting up like a squeezed balloon. His ears purpled, his hands wobbled in the air, his legs shot straight out in front of him, and his member, still protruding from his fly, grew like a squash, stretching out into the room in obscene exhibitionism, an unthinkable obscenity, a mind of its own little head, apparently. This is the way it's told.

"You bitches try to poison me," Ricky howled and a different strength took over. His clothes shredded from his limbs, hair everywhere. Ricky Romito was becoming a lupine right before their eyes. A staggeringly large wolf, and a healthy one. A wolf with a penis like a jumbo lipstick. A wolf intent it seemed sure on using aforementioned beastly member.

Selma's magic was poor stuff compared to the Boss of Beale Street's lycanthropic shapeshifting.

Callie fainted dead away.

Arms wanted so to join her but could think of no good way of depriving her brain of sufficient oxygen. The wolf licked his atrocious lips.

Now here is where the stuff of legends are made and where, I have to be honest, a few of us may part ways, apostasy accepted. There are those who do not believe in the timing of heroes, whose idea of storytelling does not extend to *deus ex machina* stunts and suchlike. So be it, I make no judgments either way. I wasn't in the room, though I was nearby, yes, and I'm just relating the way the thing has gone down now for years, in their mythopoeic way. It is strong stuff, the elixir of lore, not everyone may drink here.

I proceed.

The door again burst inward, busy door. A darkness fell upon the room, a shadow across the illumination from the overhead fixture, in the doorway, framed by unnaturally still Tillers, a numinous presence. A frozen scene: a wolf in midmolestation of a beautiful, halfnaked young woman, a passed out octogenarian, a champion standing by. The woman a hand to her vulnerable bare chest, the wolf's tongue drawing slowly up the woman's perfumed neck. The woman feeling the grip of horror slipping away, minutely, incrementally: sorrow leaving. The wolf, his lipstick rescinding, his hunger for blood on the rise. The Man.

The wolf coiled on its haunches and sprang as fast as an ejaculation.

Styx, for that's who stood in the room, a dark hero on a mission of light, held up his hand, one solid hero's hand like a papal foul call and the wolf fell to the floor as if shot. His red eyes stared upward wildly. He lay as if pinned, as if quadriplegic.

Styx let the hand stay aloft. A murkiness entered the room, a prickly heat. The air was staticky, popping and humid. A pool of spinning caloric light found its way into the upheld hand of Ygg, a puny maelstrom of power, which somehow filled the room with haboob. Ricky's pitiful stare softened Styx momentarily, the red eyes appeared to be bleeding with tears.

Styx flashed his hand downward and what looked like lightning, what possibly was lightning, blazed forth and the craven beast at their feet whimpered once and began to shrink. He went down down down, no trick of the light, a dissipating wolflet. And when he was the size of a middling walking stick, or mantis, Arms bent down and plucked him up by the minuscule scruff of his neck. He yapped and it sounded as if a triangle had been struck.

Styx reached into his cloak and pulled out an empty eight-ounce jar whose lid had already been punctured with an ice pick. Within they placed the once powerful Ricky the Rake Romito.

Some say that jar still exists downtown, in the unofficial museum of darkness in Voodoo Village. Some say the tiny figure lives on, fed on unborn mice and the droppings of flies, and that certain nights, when the moonmagic is right, he becomes again a tiny man, a tiny naked man with a Lilliputian red penis which he waves savagely at the glass much to the merriment of all, on certain moonmagic nights in Voodoo Village.

Now the rest of the plan was easy. Arms wrote the letter, the letter which they felt cleared them all, the letter designed to make it look like Ricky fled the Bluff City, hat in hand, tale between his legs, in search of other deviltry, made it look like he was gonegonegone, like the carpetbagger he was, instead of a specimen, a shrunken essence. The letter left among Ricky's abandoned things, on his desk next to his baseball signed by The Memphis Red Sox, underneath his mouthpiece from Handy's horn he used as a paperweight. Left for the authorities (who never came) to find.

Truth was nobody cared. What was the loss of such a bad egg to Beale, eternal Beale? Beale which forgave all, having seen it all. Beale with Time on its side, time and music.

Music and Time.

Toward the end of most evenings, I'm wrapping up now, like say in the penultimate number, something like "Half a Body Hoedown," or "Twist Me Up Woman" Styx would wake from a torpor of repetition and his hands would take on a new life, and the beat was like the beat at the center of things, like the lifeline number. And the crowd would dance the Vitus dance, and the drinks would exit through the sweat of the gambollers and rise up to form clouds near the cakefrosting ceiling and later, a week from then or so, it would briefly rain in Ruby's. A soft replenishing rain, empyreal confetti, which made people feel good about things, yes, if only briefly. If only for a while.

> *Arms and The Man*
>
> *on the bandstand*
>
> *"Hello Sweetcakes"*
>
> *"Hello Bacon'n'eggs"*
>
> *It was Arms it was Arms it was always Arms.*

And the new band was good, Children, fiery good. The Hammer was back and they added some strings and bassoons and the Tillers sat in most nights on washboard and kazoo. Good times.

And Arms, who stuck by the heroic drummer and gave up stripping (except on nights like this when the music swole up like a storm and she would bump and grind next to her husband's rataplan, pulling off her shirt and skirt and reminding the gathered there what was lost and what was found), who wrote the letter which she signed *annabellee yrs* and who married her drummer, was the happiest woman on Beale and beyond. Even making Callie smile from her toothless mouth, Callie who became mother to the orphan couple, Callie whom they took care of in her dotage, yes, because that's the way things were done then.

They were done right.

Santa Claus & Sam The Bartender:
A Legend

for Sam Tickle

It's a little known story, so harken:

Kris Kringle, aka Santa Claus, aka St. Nicholas (not to be confused with Nicholas of Myra called Nicholas the Wonderworker, or perhaps *to be* confused with him, the Catholic Conjuror, the patron saint of sailors...and thieves), once lived on Beale Street USA, briefly, during one of his periodic respites from the bitter cold of his arctic home. He found a place not too far from the clubs or the river, up behind a church, where he could hear, sometimes later at night than he would have anticipated, hymns being sung with a gusto put into few other human activities, wafting out into the buggy warm evening air.

When he first arrived in the preternatural Southern burg of Memphis, Tennessee, year of our Lord, 19--, he had a difficult time going out in public. No sooner would he noctambulate than he would be recognized by one or two youngsters, and he quickly became the center of a whirling mob of mankind, young and old, believers and non, eager for spoils, eager to find out more about the jolly elf than the jolly elf was willing to reveal. But, because of the temperate atmosphere of Memphis, Santa Claus began to lose weight, his ordinarily snow-white epidermis took on an amber hue, he shaved his beard like he did every off-season, and soon he could move about freely among his neighbors without being recognized. The tales of his sightings became the stuff of yellow journalism, sillier even than the latest UFO.

It was one night in one of the clubs--the Panama Hat, it might have been, the first Panama before the fire--that Santa ran into an offduty bartender named Sam, who wore the most morose countenance the Northlander had ever seen. (And not because Santa was ignorant of the blues and its phi-loss-afee, nossir, he understood, having lived and seen).

"You're the saddest sight I've seen since arriving in this fair city, friend. What ails you, tell?" Santa spoke right up, not being a shy man and being, if the truth be told, a tad supercilious about how much good he could do.

"Been way down, stranger. Don' wanna talk bout it." Sam answered, staring into his cardamon ale.

Santa pulled up a barstool without invitation.

"Reckon a sympathetic ear might do you some good. What do you imagine a newcomer like myself might have to offer an old Bealer like you when he's down in the dumps? Sympathy, friend. Empathy. Fellow feeling can't be underestimated even at the worst of times, and, who knows, I've been known to have solutions right at my fingertips. I've been known to help the downtrodden, yes I have, though I know them not to look upon. My name is Amelioration."

Sam looked at the queer, twinkly old man and snorted through his nose.

"Thas quite a speech, oldtimer, uh, Mr. Ameelorashum. I am, though, beyond aid. Thanks jus the same."

Santa laid a finger aside his nose and worked a slow smile on the woebegone bartender. Sam began to simmer under its glow. The temperature in the already steamy bar rose.

"Lord, stranger," Sam said at last. "You funny man. Ok. Whatchoo got for me?"

Santa resettled himself and grinned a whopper. This was what he lived for.

"You tell me your most private woes and I am all ears and heart and we'll see from there."

"Yas, that sounds bout right. You got time, Mr.--"

"Uh, Mr. Abovo. Klaus Abovo," Santa said, using an oft repeated pseudonym and extending a pink, puckered hand.

"Ah ha, Mr. Abovo. You got time to hear this narration?"

"All the time in the world, my good man. Shoot."

And Sam told the old man this story:

--Well az you can see I'm a white man, sir--

Santa nodded appreciatively and Sam held up a hand so the story could proceed unhindered and uncommentated upon.

--And I used to be a musician, one of the finest on Beale, if I can say so myself, playing with all the big ones, Broonzy, Mississippi Red, Styx Quetzylcoatl, the Rugrat Boys, even gigged a few times with Lady Day's band, later on now, sure, and had me my own group, called the Zouave Guard. Tight little outfit, yeah, Squiggly Robbins on the horn, Jake "Lonely Dog" Harkins, sometimes the Duchess. We was good, we was riding high.

Got us a few dollars working the weekends at PeeWees or BingoBango. Spend that money fast on that you can be sure, women, rotgut, gamblin. Well, that was the life, I sees the foolishness now but who don't lookin back?

Jake and I, we were footloose in those days, knew all the whores firstname basis and got freebies after a slow week that kind of thing. Sure they was good times for the black man on Beale, dangerous times but rightly we knew where we was.

--And here Santa opened his crystal blue eyes wide and made as if to interrupt but Sam raised his substantial hand again and shook his head and Santa settled down, assured to get to the bottom of this now-acknowledged inconsistency.

Yeah yeah, I used to be Black, Mr. Abovo. Black as Joe Louis, Black as Ricky Romito as we says around here, Black as Lady Day herself. I sees you don't believe me and I can't rightly deny it is a puzzle, but such as it is and I here to prove it.

Now bout this time I was pulled up short in my whorin ways by the prettiest woman on Beale Street, I don't mind telling you she was. She came here from Constantinople, Florida that is, and she was long and cool and the color of the delta right before a rain and all the men lay down and turned to jelly in her wake. But she was a music aficionado, Ora was, knew her jass and preciated it being played right. Well, she was there many nights at the clubs and she became our biggest fan, sittin right down front most nights and closin her big mahogany eyes and noddin in time and we all of us on the stage, even the Duchess, held her in high esteem. Long story short she took a shine to me, all the men on Beale back then and she took a shine to yours truly. I coulda died.

But me and Ora worked all right. We fit like a glove and a hand and we spent time together day and night and day again and we was at that time what you call inseparable.

First time we made love I thought I was in heaven, she sweet and smooth as Big Muddy itself and as brown and as unpredictable. She loved me good, hard and soft at the same time and I was conjurated, man, jes seein her unrobed, I--

--And here Santa squirmed a bit in his seat and Sam could see his audience was a tad uncomfortable and he hesitated and thought better of the graphic narration.

--"No, no, my man," Santa hastened to say. "I am not of prudish proclivity, not at all. I delight in all manifestations of human physical passion, championing love in its pied beauty and its myriad configurations. Yet, I can see the foreboding shadow, one might say, the presage of calamity in the angel's eye. 'Tis an oft repeated condition of man, yet 'tis as it is. Proceed, please..."

Sam took a slow swallow of his beverage and momentarily regretted regaling the old-timer with his tale of woe.

Yet he went on.

--And it was bout this time we had another fan and if Ora was sent by Heaven this one was surely the emissary of ol Scratch hisself. She was never down front near my gal, never where the light could catch her, but she was always there. I think Jake noticed her first off, scurryin on the edge of the crowd like some woodlands thing. Her eyes, he said, somethin funny bout her eyes, like the coon at night, like somethin else too.

Djoo see her? he asked me after one gig, that new fan. Pretty as a damn fire he said but unholy lookin. Hair like tree branches in wintertime--

"I jes kept catchin a glimpse of her, dancin in and outa the light, her face there in the crowd then later on somewheres else. She been there mos nights now," Jake elaborated.

And soon I started seein her too. Wild woman, gypsy woman. And it wasn't long too she come up to the stage after we played and Jake he sorta fell out and she lookin right at me, burnin me with those eyes. Portals o hell, sir.

"You play a mean blues," she say that first time.

"Yes'm," I says.

"You play as if possessed, Sam."

And I did marvel she knew my name.

"Yes'm. I learned early on from the best."

"It certainly would appear so. My name is Erin, yes?" And she extended a hand as shapely as a flame and took my big sweaty palm and I admit it now it felt like balm.

"Mayhaps you could play for me sometime?"

She drifted back into the shadow then and Ora came up and she was lookin at me askance and I sorta shrugged and went on but those eyes stayed with me, sir, and that night I dreamed a dream all fulla snakes and demons and suchlike and I woke in a sweat and Ora slept sweetly beside me and I was atremble.

She was there the next night and I say I didn't want to see her nohow but truth be told somethin in me wanted her to take my hand again and I think now she was already workin her negromancy on me. But then I jes thought I was struck with her and felt a bit guilty bout Ora and all. And that night she requested me to play this here party she was throwin and she said it was to be that Saturday night and I said well we were giggin at Bingo that night and she said no mind this would be later. And furthermore this here party was to be out in the woods south of here in the river bottoms and was to be out under the full moon and it was a celebration of some sort and that we would be paid royally.

Well the band said they thought not and I was rightly agreed with them but she looked at me so mournfully and I says well maybe jes I could come if she didn't mind a oneman band and she says naw that would be jes fine. I used to play jes me you see and I had me a single act was well respected and I could play mos blues with jes my guitar and that seemed to be what she wanted anyhow.

That night Ora she wasn't too keen on me playin for this wild woman and she was in a huff and turned away from me and I lay lookin at the ceiling all night and thinkin and what I was thinkin I ashamed to say but honesty and the integrity of the story requires I do so. And it was this:

I was sexually fantasizin bout this witch-woman and it seemed so real I don know whether maybe I slipped into a dream or so but she was there with me and twined about my legs like some seductive cat and I could feel her up the lengtha my legs and all my hairs standin on end and I come on myself and in burnin shame I had to get up and go wash off in the bathroom there while my angel slept on unawares.

So the next day I looked for this Erin to tell her I ain't playin no party in the woods and I was bound and determine to tell her to quit showin up at our gigs. And while we was playin, and that night we weren't quite up to snuff the music soundin like we was all playin different songs and nothin was comin out right and I kept thinkin I sees her from the stage, here the side of her face with that wild hair splayed out, over there her eyes jes behind some college boy and again in the corner there movin her lips to the song and her mouth drawin me in. It was all I could do to concentrate and when the set was over I was glad and jumped down off that stage. But I never found her that night, she musta left early.

Saturday night came round and Ora she been cold shoulderin me and makin me mad and I determined I didn't care nohow and was gonna play that party in the woods and pocket that specie and get me good and drunk on it and maybe not come home till I was numb.

And when the boys and me finished that night there
out of the murk stepped Erin with her dark bristly eyes and
her willowy body and she slithered up to me and took my
hand and I was long gone man, I'da followed her anywhere.

Outside she led me to a waiting car and we gots in
the back seat and she introduced me to the driver who was
this wormy lookin little white guy name of Dwight and he
kept sniggerin like he knew some joke no one else knew and
I couldn't rightly attend to him anyways cuz this witchy
woman was rubbin my chest and sidlin up to me with her long
cool smoothness and my head was swimmin.

Long and short was we went way out down into
Mississippi maybe and the road curved this way and that and
the night was cool and moonlit and the moon seemed to glow
hot up there obliteratin the stars and we came to this wide
open field and there was much merriment and deviltry goin
on already and it looked as if this was a party in full swing
and we was late arrivin. At first it seemed to be a crowd
of foreigners, folks I ain't never seen before on Beale or
elsewhere, all dressed like animals with antlers on their heads
and skins and feathers everywhere and I think it was jes my
fatigue makin me see things cuz soon I began to recognize
folks here and there and it seemed there was mos everybody I
ever known or wished to.

They was all there, guys I played with in the past,
gals I once knew and some few I didn't care to see no more
but it didn't matter none. It was a sanctified gatherin: Red
Rolly, Shoeboot Reeder, Lyle Talbot, Shlomo "Einstein" Stern,
Magpie Skinner, J. Howard Griffin, the Beetle Brothers,
Antenna Rogers. I swear I seen kith I ain't seen in years, some
I thought had done passed on to their glory. Someone was
whisperin Mr. Handy hisself was there but I didn't pay that
no mind though now it don't seem so farfetched.

--And here Santa stood up and stretched his short
legs and had a countance that was grim and troubled. Sam
paused in his recitation and ordered another round and the

elfish stranger rubbed his stubbly chin and looked at Sam with sweet sympathy.

"I'm much concerned by this tale and can see somewhat where it is pointing. Are you certain you wish to continue its telling as I believe it is the basis for no small amount of suffering?"

And Sam nodded with warm assurance.

I'm thankin you for your consideration. But now I feel I mus proceed--

--They had fashioned theyselves a makeshift stage and after some time I stepped up onto it and the crowd grew quiet and their faces peered up at me from the stillness of the surroundin night and I was sore afraid and froze up there for the first time in my career.

Now Erin seein this hesitating stepped up near me and ran her silky palm over my cheek and put her soft full lips onto mine and kissed me long and humid and locked her eyes onto mine and I lifted my guitar and I began to play.

I started with some standards, some tunes I always warmed up with, somethin familiar, some goin way back, fife and drum blues and "Mississippi Lowdown" and "Up the Rooster Road" and "Write Em Right" and the congregation was into it and their faces swarmed around me shapeshiftin and swayin and I was as if hypnotized. I began to play harder sweatin and beatin on my guitar as if I hated it and loved it, the passion swellin in me fit to bust outa my chest.

And I don know if it was the negromancy or the moonmagic or the patronage of the crowd but I was playin things I ain't never heard of before, music from the beginning, devil's tunes. I was playin the music from *before*, some deep down blues come outa man's soul and healin and wreakin havoc all at once and I was all ways possessed. I was singin bout love and hate and I was damned to explain it all and the feelin came up from the folks gathered there and went through me and returned back to from where it came. And I was slashin my guitar and the guitar wasn't even there and the music continued and it answered the night and I was all alone in the wilderness cryin and playin.

And it happened that night. I could feel the feelin flowin through me and I was playin my heart out and like the heat was leavin my body I could feel myself bein drained and the night was growin darker and the moon disappearin and the energy was rollin outa me and I musta swooned.

I woke and it was mornin and I was alone with my guitar gone too and I was as if naked and the negromancy had been done and I was as white as you see me now. I done played the black outa me.

I walked back slowly to Beale Street and I was hungover-like and it took me all day to make that cheerless trek and that night I stumbled into my bed and Ora was nowheres aroun and I fell asleep and dreamed I was the last man in the world and I had no voice and it didn't matter nohow and I could sing inside my head but nothin came out and I wept in my dream and when I awoke there were tears on my face and it was another day.

Long and short was no one recognized me and my gal took up with another bluesman, a new guy in town who played, they said, as if he was Robert Johnson's bastard and Ora wouldna even look at me disdainin white men as she did rightly or wrongly and the band said yeah yeah they believed I was Sam their compatriot but I could see they didn't and I was mos alone.

I told them jes to hear me play and I borrowed a guitar and you know I could still hit the same chords and I could still move my fingers in the same dex-terous way and my voice could still sing with all the notes jes so but somethin was missin. Somethin was missin. And the boys jes grinned sympathetically and said sure I was good but I could see I was through as a bluesman.

I tried everthing I could think of to change me back.
Went to see a conjure woman, dunked myself in the Big
Muddy repeatedly. It was no good, I had been hexed and
hexed good.

I wandered the streets for a while like some ancient
mariner but I could not tell my tale till this night and I was a
debauch an a sponge an worse and I finally got me a job at the
Bingo as a barkeep where I serve the hootch but don't drink it
nomore and hear the stories told dolefully but do not recount
my own. Til this night.

And thas the way it is and why I'm the saddest man
on Beale and everybody knows my name and I jes Sam the
Bartender now. Sometimes I hear tell the stories of Sam the
Bluesman who could play like Apollo and how he disappeared
and all and the mystery is still alive but I jes wash the glasses
and wipe the bar and smile my smile, cuz I know the truth.

--Now Santa could not look up into the face of his new
confidant for a few moments and he surreptitiously wiped a
tear away and swallowed the last of what was in his glass and
he looked into the middle distance for a while.

Sam thought his story had fallen on deaf ears until the
old man turned and he could see the understanding there and
he was heartened.

Santa spoke first.

"This story much grieves me, for I know the ways of
magic and do hate to see them misused for evil intent. This
Erin, I am sure, has not shown her face long since."

"That is a fack, friend," Sam said.

"And I know no way to reverse this spell," the old man
said as if he thought it in his ken to deliver the sorrowful
barkeep.

"Mr. Abovo, I preciate the intent but I am beyond the ways of men. Bein white isn't so bad, pardon me for sayin it so, and I have adjusted to the world without my true love and my music."

"Should not be so," Mr. Abovo muttered as he rose and reached into his pocket for payment for the night's libations.

"Put your jack away, sir," Sam said. "They know me here and it is taken care of."

"I'm grateful, Sam. And I will ponder on this dilemma and hope to see you again in my peregrinations."

"Don worry your head, Mr. Abovo. The way it is is the way it is."

And Santa went back to his apartment that night and he could hear the hymns swaying out into the chill night air muffled as if wafting all the way from Elysium and he stayed up a while and made a few phone calls and slept but little.

The next night at the club Sam was stirring the drinks with a new lightness which he did wonder at. It is the unburdening of telling my tale, he decided and some say the story ends here and Sam lived not so happily ever after but not so bad either, the examined life and all and he possessed a profound understanding of things which is given to few mortals.

But another version goes like this:

One night at BingoBango he was serving up the Zombi Killers as usual and some sidewinder in a cowboy outfit came in and bellowed out something about being a coward and squeezed off a few rounds from his sixguns into the ceiling before being coldcocked and after the commotion died down Sam noticed somebody new sitting at his bar, somebody decidedly new, who studied her surroundings like a student of the world and rested her fresh pearly eyes on Sam and smiled a slight earthshattering smile in his general direction and Sam gamboled over to offer his services.

She was as white as the snows of the North and her hair the color of cornsilk and she looked like the answer to a question Sam puzzled over sometime in his oh-so distant past. And Sam the Bartender knew something slowly as he stood in front of her and then he knew it with his heart though his head understood it not. It was Ora and she was as white as flour and she had come back for him. It was a miracle. It was a benediction.

"Cardamon ale," the white woman whispered, and the rest is history.

They married and had children and their children lived to see Beale die and be reborn and Sam sometimes sang to them songs from long ago, songs the slaves sang, songs of love and hate, songs the world grew up knowing.

Jack Crosswaith & The Devil:
A Children's Story

❝ Jack Crosswaith and the Devil" is based on an African-American folktale which appears in Zora Neale Hurston's **Mules & Men** as "How Jack Beat the Devil."

There lived on Beale Street in those days a man as big as a parson's barn, a man who could step across the Mississippi River without dunking his boots. A man with the strength of love, the strength of death, and his name was Jack Crosswaith.

Now, Jack worked most days down at Club BingoBango, during the days lifting the piano or bar so they could sweep under them and most nights he just stood around like a thunderstorm, preventing trouble just by his larger-than-life presence.

Tales abound about Jack.

They say he once barbecued a whole cow by holding it over a fire with his bare hands.

They say he once used the Harahan Bridge for a back-scratcher.

They say he fought Wild Bill Latura and nearly killed him with the first punch but Wild Bill was a tough man himself and the two fought for three days and nights and eventually concluded not out of fatigue but because Mr. Handy walked in and the place went as still as a church.

They say he drank rain storms and blinked lightning.

Now, Jack's best friend, in those days, was a bluesman name of Sweetie Sykes. Sweetie had played with all of them but was probably best known for blowing horn with Bob Miller and his Syncopaters. Sweetie was a prince back then; few of us can understand today.

Sweetie brought out the best in Jack Crosswaith and his music soothed the savage beast in the broad-shouldered giant. Not that Jack had that much of a temper. He was a noble man, but maybe too strong for his own good.

Sweetie sang some as well as played his horn and wrote some fine tunes in his day. Some of the legends about Jack survive because of Sweetie's songs, for this is how legends stay alive, spread from bar to bar, from juke joint to juke joint, from dancing hall to living room to classroom.

There's the ballad, "Jack C. and the Frizzly Rooster." There's "Jack's Elegy." And there's the famous blues with its irresistible lyrics:

> De snow is cold, de wind does blow
>
> De snow is cold, de wind does blow
>
> But Jack's the strongest man I know
>
> Heaven's above, hell's down below
>
> Heaven's above, hell's down below
>
> But Jack's the strongest man I know

It was this song that Sweetie was singing at BingoBango the night old Scratch himself came in. That same night the Duchess was sitting in with the band, playing her old shoebox guitar, and behind the bar was the original Sam the bartender and the new kid, Huck, was acting as bouncer in Jack's absence. Jack wasn't there and no one rightly recollects why--some say he was up in the north part of the state digging a hole that was to be called Reelfoot Lake.

Anyway, it was late and everything was pretty slow and smoky, like a dream, and in walked Scratch--that is, the Devil himself--with two of his henchman, a squatty little horntoad name of Roofus and a skinny snakeoil salesman he called Pic.

They sat in the back at a table by themselves and nobody paid them much mind, what with the long, lazy notes the band was putting out and all. They weren't bothering anybody, at first.

After the band finished that set Sweetie went to the bar and was ordering himself a Rub of the Brush when the Devil sauntered over.

He stuck out a long-fingered hand, like the hand a lizard might have, and introduced himself this way:

"Pleased to make your acquaintance, Bluesman. My name is Mr. Nick."

"I know who you is," Sweetie said without turning his head.

"Indeed," the Devil said.

"I saw you with my friend, Robert Johnson."

"Ah, yes," Old Scratch said, looking seriously at the bluesman's profile.

"You want something of me, Mr. Nick?" Sweetie asked. "Cuz I'm satisfied with my lot in life and I ain't about to sell my soul for no extra bit of talent."

"Quite so," the Devil said. "That song you sang, I wanted to ask you about it."

"Sang me lots of songs, Mr. Nick," Sweetie answered.

"Yes, the one about Jack particularly interests me however," Old Nick said, as sickly sweet as could be.

Sweetie turned now and looked the Devil in his serpentine eyes. "Jack's the strongest man I know. He usually here but not tonight. If he were he'd toss your sorry self outside just for looking cross."

The minor demons snickered but were silenced by a fiery look from Mr. Nick.

"So you say," the Devil said.

"It's so."

"And I'd wager half my kingdom that it is not. That is, that I could best your friend Jack in any test of physical strength you could devise."

"And if you win?" Sweetie wanted to know.

"Then I take Jack with me back to my, ahem, place of business."

Sweetie was still for a long moment. The crowd in BingoBango were still as if spellbound.

"I'll take that bet," Sweetie said finally.

The day of the big duel was a bright, hot day on Beale Street. The sun was directly overhead and the sides of the streets were lined with the curious and the crazy.

Most of the bets had Jack besting the Devil; he was a 2 to 1 favorite. Some were not confident, though, and there were doubts expressed as to whether any mortal man, even a man as powerful as local hero Jack, could scrap with Old Nick.

Jack, however, never expressed any doubt. When Sweetie told him of the wager he smiled broadly and patted his friend on the back.

"It's as good as done," Jack said.

The Devil arrived with his two wormy henchmen by his side. He swaggered as he moved down the crowded street. He smiled from left to right, showing the assembled multitudes the kind of easy grace with which he ran his evil empire.

He greeted Jack in the middle of Beale with a scaly hand extended.

"Sir," the Devil said, "I have heard much of you."

"And I of you," Jack said, taking the Devil's paw in his large meaty hand and holding on with the grip of an iron vise. The Devil returned the pressure and the two stood in the bright sun glaring at each other, squeezing each other for all they were worth.

After some time it seemed to be agreed that neither would get the better of the other this way.

They stepped a few feet apart and the contest began.

Old Nick took a horseshoe and bent it straight. He handed it to Big Jack. Jack took it and bent it back into a horseshoe.

The crowd applauded.

The Devil then took a chain as thick as a man's arm and broke it in two as if it were kindling.

Jack did the same with the remaining sections of chain.

This went on for some time. The strength of one was matched by the strength of the other.

Both of them split trees with single punches. Both broke boulders against their foreheads. Both bent railroad spikes with their teeth.

After two hours the crowd was tired from clapping but the two contestants were not even winded. They glared at each other.

"This could go on all day and night," Sweetie finally declared.

"What do you propose?" the Devil looked at the Bluesman out of slit eyes.

"Jack?" Sweetie asked his friend.

Jack looked the Devil up and down. He studied carefully the hammer the Devil was carrying at his waist, a thing forged from the inner earth, a thing as dark and diabolic as the creature carrying it.

"That hammer," Jack said, nodding at the Devil's waist.

"What of it?" the Devil said, instinctively putting a protective hand on it.

"Let's see who can throw it the farthest."

The Devil was caught for a moment.

"This hammer is quite dear to me, with it I built the Stygian stables," he said. After a pause he added, "But we may use it for this wager. You have spelled out your own doom, Big Man, for this hammer is almost part of me and I will surely better you in any contest involving it."

"Let us see," Jack said. "You may throw first."

The Devil removed the hammer from his side and weighed it in his hand. He looked around at the people on both sides of the street and smiled a sinister, smoky smile.

"It is Tuesday now," the Devil announced to the crowds on Beale. "I shall throw this hammer in the air and it will not descend until Thursday morning at nine o'clock. You may set your watches by it."

And he heaved it into the sky.

The assembled congregation watched it disappear into the clouds. Sweetie watched it disappear into the clouds. Jack watched it disappear into the clouds.

Everyone stood looking skyward for a long time. One by one the people began to mutter and walk away. Soon it was only Jack, Sweetie, and the three bogies in the street.

"I will see you again on Thursday," the Devil said and, in a puff of sulfurous smoke, the demons were gone.

Sweetie spent a couple of sleepless nights worrying about what he had gotten Jack into. That was a powerful throw and he had no confidence that his friend could better the Devil with his own tool.

On stage he was so discombobulated he played poorly those two nights and the audiences were restless and without enthusiasm. Club BingoBango was as sad as a thousand sighs. Few believed Jack could beat the Devil's throw.

Thursday morning people were lining the streets as early as seven a.m. If anything there were more people there than on Tuesday, for word of the contest had spread into Mississippi and Arkansas.

At a quarter to nine the unholy trio sauntered down Beale and greeted the crowd with smiles and tipped hats.

Boos and hisses resulted, for most believed the Devil was soon to spirit their beloved Jack away from them.

Jack smiled.

At eight fifty-nine someone on the side of the street pointed upward and, sure enough, a speck could be seen in the great expanse of blue. It was the hammer falling from space.

At precisely nine a.m. the hammer hit the middle of Beale Street with a resounding crack, sank one hundred yards into the earth and shook the ground for a full thirty seconds.

The Devil looked at Jack and Jack looked at the Devil. The Devil held out his hand and the hammer rose from its cavity and flew right into Old Nick's bony hand.

"Your throw," the Devil said.

Jack took the hammer from the Devil and held it in his hand. He looked around him at the sea of faces, anxiously awaiting some deliverance from their doubts. He looked at his friend Sweetie and he smiled a smile as broad as the summer day.

He bent low and uncoiled his body in a monstrous rush, hurling the hammer into the air with every bit as much power as the Devil had exhibited on the previous Tuesday.

Everyone watched the hammer disappear one more time.

"Well," the Devil said, slyly. "When, pray tell, will your throw descend?"

Jack waited one devilish moment.

"It won't," he said.

"It won't?" the Devil said.

"I threw it into Heaven," Jack said.

The Devil stood in the middle of Beale Street and sweat began to form on his beetle-y brow. He looked from henchman to henchman. He looked at the faces lining the street. He looked back at the sky.

"Move over, Gabriel. Stand back, Jesus," Jack said, calmly.

"Hold on," the Devil sputtered. "You can't have done that. I, I left a whole mess of tools up there when they kicked me out. I can't go back there yet."

Jack just smiled.

"My hammer," the Devil wailed. "My precious hammer."

The Devil hesitated one more second and then with a whoosh like a powerful firework he shot heavenward, followed in a clumsy surge by his two befuddled confederates.

After that Beale Street pretty much went back to its business. Jack still worked at BingoBango most days and Sweetie began playing with a new relish and writing more songs than ever. Sweetie now officially owned half the Devil's kingdom, but he never paid it no mind. He wasn't a greedy man and just wanted his blues and his friends and the peace of long summer nights at the gateway to the Delta.

The Devil, it is said, eventually got back from heaven and continued his fiendish ways, but he never, as far as anyone knows, went near Beale Street again.

HUCK & HOMINY:
AN EPISTOLARY ROMANCE

Badly missing someone depopulates a world."

Alexander Theroux

*It is necessary to cross the bridges
and to reach the black murmur,
so that the perfume of lungs strike our temples
with its suit of warm pineapple."*

Federico Garcia Lorca

Dear Gumboots,

Yesterday evening at sunset the river must have been on fire the color of the bars and buildings purred so. It was still so hot even after the sun went down and the air seemed to be full of electricity and water as if such a thing were possible, the river was a real presence on the street last night I know you know what I mean. I know you remember. It was a reminder as if I needed one that you were not here and it made me remember similar nights when the weather would carry us out into the street with a drink or a rib or such in our hands and we would stroll westward among the lively and life was so full of possibilities, I know you felt that too.

What's it like in Cincinnati, I can't even imagine. Is there music there? Is there colored folk? Do you like the job you took with the paper company, do they treat you nice?

At the club things are hot, so hot they hired a new girl named Callie. She's a stripper not just a waitress like myself and she is luscious and I guess I wish you could see her appreciator that you are of the feminine graces. She has skin like a Mississippi milkshake and the men fairly give up their seed when she first steps onto the runway. Mr. Burro I reckon likes her act and the money she is bringing our way.

This weekend you know is Cotton Makers and we're gussying up for that and putting on extra help and a few more guns and made a few deals on cutrate booze and I don't know if we'll be ready or not. I don't think so but I feel that way every year and it works out all right.

Except this year you're not here.

Oh, Huck. I don't know about this. I'm trying to be good like you asked and talk of other things, just bringing you news off the street, just making my life appear normal or something. It ain't working.

You know I don't understand this "trial separation"
thing, I don't follow. Mama said you were too modern with
all that schooling and stuff and that psychology falala. Does
absence really make the heart grow fonder, I don't think so.
My heart hurts I mean it literally hurts like my accelerator's
stuck. And I can't sleep.

I'm gonna have to close this before I get too carried
away. I'm not pressuring you or anything, I'm fine really. I
miss you is all and I know we'll get through this and you'll be
back here as soon as soon. Mr. Burro said you could have your
old job back anytime.

Give my love to your cousin Alligator.

yours and you know it
Hominy

Dear Honey-Hominy,

Oh you know I miss you too, Sweetcakes. I can't describe to you the world inside my head or make it any clearer but I know I just KNOW that this is for the best. Bear with me. You know I love you.

The job at Cuttermeyer's is a good job and has large chances for a young man to improve himself and Mr. Cuttermeyer has his eye on me I think I can tell already. He tipped his hat my way this morning and all I was doing was tying up stacks of boxes. A man can get attention tying boxes is a man bound for the good life is the way I'm looking at that.

Cuttermeyer's daughter Laurie works here, well in the office. Short butt-y little white woman with the requisite turned up nose and small spray of freckles and a mop of black curls, athletic legs all thigh and muscle and nothing on the top, not like you baby. Ohh I miss those amplenesses. And Laurie Cuttermeyer herself came down yesterday and smiled my way and said to the other men there so that her daddy and everyone could hear, "We should all work as hard as Huck here and maybe we wouldn't be heading for insolvency."

Well it made me proud and no doubt. If this works out for me here, well, I can't say now, but we'll have to see.

Glad to hear the club is doing well. I miss the boys and the stripshows and that lowdown house sound the BamBams concocted. I miss my drink, my Rub of the Brush. I miss Mississippi Sam Peeps and his steel doing "I Used to Be Black but I Lost the Knack."

Mostly I miss you and your cocoa thighs and your nipples like grapes and the way you say "oh heavenly host" and squinch your eyes up tight when you coming.

This is gonna work out, Honey. We were getting stale together, going nowhere, stuck inside of Memphis and weighed down by the heat and the blood in our eyes. This resting time is gonna be the cure. Count on me.

Alligator sends his love back at you.

I'm your sugar-man.

love you betcha
Huck

Dear Huck Honey,

It was so good to get your letter and the reassurance and I read that letter three times and then took it to bed with me and in the morning read it one more time. My new friend Callie (did I tell you about her, she works at the club now?) came over and I read the letter to her and she's all cynical and all but she allowed as to how you sounded like a good man underneath.

The Jubilee was as crazy as ever and I didn't get to bed that night or none the next day until 2 in the afternoon but Mr. Burro said I was the backbone of the business and gave me an extra twenty for the sweat of it. We flat ran out of booze about midmorning and started selling the hootch Old Riverbones makes in his flatboat and that went over well and all told on Beale only a half dozen negroes died in gunfights and elsewise. Not a bad year overall.

One crazy black man from Shaw Miss. got out into the middle of the street about midnight and fired his revolver into the air straight toward heaven and the bullet went straight up and came straight back down and pierced his skullcap and he's dead.

The crowds on the street that night were overwelling and it was a variable sea of black and everybody was there, Red Rolly, Bertah from Biloxi, Arty Shaw, Wild Bill Latura, Chuck the Knife, Axle Concertina, Styx, Sam, all the women you ever bedded, your cousin Lampedusa, the Greenville Gang, and that Loup Garou from the Clubs, skulking around, and it was quite a sight. Huck it was all meaningless without you. I mean I looked out on that congest and I couldn't see anybody like I was blind and the world had whited out. Like that quick second after the flashbulb done burst.

I ain't going on again. Mama says you're coming back when you're rich and ready. I'm horny without you.

I'm flesh-lonely.

Write again real quick I need your letters to feel you
here.

Real love and all.
        Hominy

Dear Honey-Hominy,

Sorry I hadn't written sooner. I been so busy here the box factory is going great guns and they're talking about putting on some extra folk and making some promotions.

I found a little club near work where the music isn't so bad and they let negroes cut up a little without calling the law so quick. I've been spending some nights there, me and Alligator and some others.

I'll send some money back soon as I can. I ran into a little trouble with the rent but I'll get that straightened and be on easy street soon. Bet on it. Laurie says I'm on my way.

I'll write back soon as I get some more time.

love,
Huck

Dear Huck-honey,

Your letter found me longing for you and hungry for
news and I read that sucker must have been twenty times. (It
was easy you didn't have much to say I guess.) (Just teasing,
but write more, do.). The Club is still working me till my
back aches but Mr. Burro says the sales are down some. I
don't know, seems like we been busy enough most nights.
Sometimes though there's just me and Cal and Burt the
Bartender (I forget you don't know Burt he took your place,
well he took the place of the guy who took your place (Cal
says he's hung like a painting but you probably don't want
to hear that) after you split though he's no Huck Mr. Burro's
fond of saying) and the place seems like an empty galaxy.

Oh Huck, Bessie Smith came through last week, a few
days after Cotton Makers I guess it was. Came right into our
club, sat down front, listened to the music for a while (it was
Old Mama Redbone and I do believe she was so nervous at
having the lady herself down front she kept forgetting the
words and making up her own and some of the things she
came out with were a downright hoot I tell you) and when
she got up to leave, with her man on her arm, the whole place
stood and clapped, you never seen anything like it. It was
royalty was what it was.

I wished you could have been there.

Aw Huck. I want to see you. I will learn to live with
the fact that I can't. I am lost in you and I guess I've got to
find my way out.

Please write me soon as I live for your letters.

your honeydo,
Hominy

Dear Honey,

Don't worry about the club. It'll work out. That club's a Beale club and it'll be there when the rapture comes. Count on it.

My job here is still ok. Things are a little slow.

I got a new address I'll have to give it to you. The old place wasn't working out so good.

This new club I been going to is interesting. The other night the band played "Wiggling Harper Blues" and I thought of you. That's the song you used to carry on so much about, isn't it? It was something like that.

I hadn't seen Alligator in some time. I think he moved up east.

I'm working on some things. I'll be back in touch real quick. Don't carry on so, sugar.

Huck

Dear Huck,

    I cannot function when I am at the mercy of despair--
truly I cannot eat, or work, or talk; I lose the desire to go on.

    You will tire of my discouragement I know. I don't
really know what to say. I'm anxious, angst-ridden, angry
even. I have a lot of things to figure out. Maybe I should be a
fatalist like Mama.

    The club seems so dead these days, the whole of Beale.
I swear sometimes it's a ghost town here. There are rumblings
among the club owners about declining business; some talk
of moving on, up east, and elsewhere. Last week we had a few
days where no one came in, No One. The new bartender was
out sick and it didn't matter and it made the club seem like an
empty cell.

    The Club was my world, was where I lived. Without
the Club am I dead? Oh and you were my world, Huck
and the club, used to be one thing. Used to be The Thing.
Hominy's reason for being.

    I go home nights and my house doesn't recognize me.
My things all piled up and useless, someone else's things. I
walk around like a survivor after a war, pick up a phonograph
record or a spoon and look at it and it all seems so strange.
No one calls, no one comes by. Callie has left the club and
is stripping in New Orleans, I believe she said. I ain't heard
from her.

    Sorry to sound so down, honey. Please please write
soon.

love and delicious tongue kisses,

Hominy

Dear Hominy,

Sorry to be so long writing. Been on the move.

I need to talk to you, explain some things. About me
and Laurie. About me.

Don't worry.
Huck

Huck,

What's going on? It's so long between letters and then this half-finished card. What about you and Laurie? What about us? Oh, Huck. Come back to Beale. Come back soon.

If Beale is still here, I mean, I think the street's dying, baby. Days go by and I see no one. Mr. Burro has shut down the club, he says temporarily. Temporarily means no money.

I need you, Huck honey. Please let me know soon when you can come back, things aren't good here. I want to hold you. I need your hands and your breath on my neck...you take it from there. Please.

I feel like if you came back everything would be all right. This is fantasy I know. But it's all so empty without you, maybe if you were here, the club would come alive again, you were always so popular. Huck, I'm losing everything.

Write and tell me when you can come see me. We need to get together, we can make it good again, I swear.

I love you.
your Honey

Dear Huck,

It's been three weeks. I can't do this alone. I can't keep this up from my end alone.

Where are you? With you gone the world is abandoned for me. Please just write and tell me you're ok.

Beale Street is dead. All the bars are closed. I can't even find Mr. Burro to ask about BingoBango. I'm hungry.

It's so lonely here. I haven't seen another living soul for days, maybe longer. I'm losing weight. The world's losing weight.

I need to hear from you.

Hominy

Dear Huck,

I swear if I could get to Cincinnati I would come there and recover you. I realize now you ain't gonna write me back.

Your life goes on without me.

Are you ok? Do you ever get lonely?

Huck, remember the good times.

Please, come find me.
Hominy

Dear Huck,

The leaves are falling off all the trees on our street. That ginkgo we loved is dying, I think, something other than seasonal departure at work down in its roots. I love Memphis because of all the trees and autumn always makes me a little sad, as if all my friends were changing or moving on without me. It's just a cycle Mama used to say, God's plan for constant renewal.

If it wasn't for the trees and the cooler winds I wouldn't know where we are in the year. My calendar still says June and I haven't had the initiative to change it and now I've lost track and wouldn't know where to pick up again.

I found a new handbill in the street today, one I haven't seen before, advertising some new act I hadn't heard of, playing at some club I hadn't heard of. At first I thought it was a sign of new life, someone with a little hope moving here with a plan to set things up and get something going again. But it had blown here from somewhere else, somewhere beyond the river maybe, maybe from Cincinnati. Maybe it's from the club where you go, maybe it's someone you know.

Nothing else is new on the street these days. All the buildings look grey and useless and the paint's flaking on the signs and the posters all are for shows and folks long gone. Sometimes I walk outside from one end of Beale to the other and maybe I see Old Riverbones, maybe I see nobody. A few days ago, how many I don't know, Old Riverbones stopped me and asked me my name. It's only cause he's getting old I guess, I guess he knows me about as well as anybody. We talked a few minutes about the old days and he seemed a little confused--Time is all skimble-skambled in his head--it's what happens to the mind, to the world-- and allowed as to how he was probably moving on himself, up river he said, and I would've laughed except it struck me as kind of sad.

Mama died. They took her body up east to where her family is. I couldn't go.

This morning I went out to look around. I was getting the heebie-jeebies sitting around that apartment with the walls getting blanker and more threatening and I had to rush out for a breath of air.

I walked down to Beale and wandered in and out of doorways, looked into grimy windows and shady doors. Stood for a while outside the pawn shop and tried to make out each item there, left abandoned and unwanted. I went over to BingoBango and stood in the entranceway and looked through the glass and the tables were all standing there ready as if the show was going on tonight. Remember, Huck that night Mr. Handy was playing and you were tending bar and I was just a newcomer there all nervous and hoping for big tips. And that white woman was coming on to you and you were so cool back there--all the gals wanted you--and you had your eyes on me and we were sort of locked into each other and we knew it and little had to be said. That white woman just wandered away all sadeyed and I came up to that bar later and you said Your name Honey and I didn't want to embarrass you and said Yes Yes my name's Honey and for a long time that's all you called me, for a goodly time after that.

I thought I heard somebody in the back of BingoBango and I tapped lightly on the glass but I knew it was just a rat or something. Nobody's been in there for months.

It was so quiet it was the end of the world.

I meandered down the street, moving pointlessly, and it struck me like a revelation. Everybody's gone. Everybody isn't here anymore, and I tried to remember when the last time I had seen another human being was and I couldn't do it. There are no more people.

And I stood there in the middle of Beale and I started crying and I let those tears fall all the way down, down onto the street. I cried a river, I let my tears flow down to Beale and I was crying for the losses, for the loss of the world, for the old lonely world. I wept for the heartache in all of us. I wept for the empty spaces, for the ends of things. I wept for the way things were and the way things won't be no more.

And I stood there alone on that spot and I figured I just had to go on home and a wind started blowing, a murmuring wind with musical undertones. There's no one anywhere and the wind's blowing down Beale, and it sounded like old voices.

I love you.
Hominy

WRITE EM RIGHT:
A COLLOQUY

I remember the way it was.

I remember.

Not so many of us left now.

Count em on one hand. Specially my hand.

Roman Rebus, Old Willy Lowman, the Jones brothers, Squeaky Joint and Gooseneck, Blind Pete, the Shawcross brothers.

Annie Divine, Red Rolly...

He dead.

Rolly dead?

The cancer. Last year.

Declare.

Taken some good ones. Taken some heels.

Ha. Lou Washboard Miller, Hank the Horn, Seven Finger Tucker...

Thas me.

Jus sayin. You still with us.

Yes. For a little while longer. Yourself.

Well... That white boy, sang like a big bander, deep voice.

Don' know who you mean.

Big guy, gassed back hair, white hair almos'. Sang "Chicken Finger Blues." Sang "Write Em Right."

"Mississippi Lowdown Blues."

That was Guy Jimmy, dead these sixteen years. Dead of the drink.

Yes.

Fucked Big Bill's gal, skinny do nothin.

Bill shot him, oh yeah. Bill shot him till he was dead.

Whas his name?

Don' know.

You know him.

Nope.

Hillbilly somethin'.

You thinkin a Hillbilly Thomas. Not the same cat. Hillbilly sang with Big Bill, played slide with a thimble. Died a broken man, died in Philly.

Naw.

I'm tellin you.

How he die?

Broken.

You said that. How?

Woman took off on him, couden play no more, voice gone.
Sat down an died. I'm told.

Huh. Didden know.

Yeah.

So whom I thinkin of?

Who?

Big white guy, gassed back hair. Sang "Write Em Right." Sang
"The Gal Messed Me Up, She Messed Me Up Good."

Don' know that one.

What?

That las one. "The Gal Messed Me Up..."

You know it.

Naw.

"The gal messed me up.

 She messed me up good.

 The gal messed me up.

 She messed me up good.

 Well, that gal messed me up..."

You know.

Don' recollect it.

Tucker. You righteous fool.

Right, right. You playin? You playin tonight?

Hah. Where dat be? Newby's? Club 666? They gonna open those doors wide for me. You?

Got me a gig.

You don' say.

Sure. Playin at a church, a white church.

Yeah.

Payin. Thas what I know. Wanna resurrect the ol days, they say. Wanna make up for the in-justice. I say, you payin?

Ha. Yeah, yeah. You need backin? You need somebody?

Aw, don' need nobody, Mister. You hurtin?

Naw. Itchin to play is all.

You got your guitar?

I get one.

Sure. Yeah, sure. You come play with me, you come tonight, Mister.

You sure?

Sure. Yeah.

What you know?

The ol ones, the good tunes.

You doin "Silver Dollar"? You doin "Her Ass Moves I Moan"?

I ain't doin Her Ass, naw. I do "Silver Dollar."

Good, good.

You wanna get somethin to eat? You hungry?

Sure. Where to?

Mickey's wife always cookin.

So I hear.

Haw, haw. You right there.

White Bobby Hawkins.

Who dat?

White Bobby Hawkins. The cat with the hair, the big white guy.

Not to be confused with Black Bobby Hawkins.

Thas the guy.

Sang "Write Em Right."

Yeah.

He dead.

Naw.

Yeah, the blood or somethin. Dead long time.

Huh.

Thought you said Bill shot him?

Thas some other guy.

You hungry?

Yeah, I could eat.

Wanna go to Mickey's.

Mickey aint' there. Mickey, he's in Cincinnati.

Yeah.

Haw, haw.

Wanna go now.

Sure. Sure now.

BUTTERFLY McQUEEN'S OSCAR:
A LIE

> **❝** *Although little of it remains physically, there is still much to talk about.* ❞
>
> Richard Raichelson
> from *Beale Street Talks*

A NECESSARY PART OF THE HISTORY

As far as I know, the story of Butterfly McQueen's Oscar has never before been told. Its veracity is dubious as hell, but its half-baked quality--part raw hyperbole and part overdone mythmaking--make it a necessary part of the history. I mean everyone's history, but most especially, and what we'll deal with here, the convoluted taletelling told of Resole McRey.

Now Resole was a fixture on the Street, as natural a phenomenon as the flood, as common an accessory as dusky bluesmen with too much past and no presence, halfheartedly strumming out-of-tune guitars in Handy Park. He was ubiquitous, mercurial, out of step but plugged in, simultaneously an insider and the world's best outsider.

No one knows where he came from and, in the end, no one knows where he went. But that's the end. Let's go chronologically.

Resole was a storyteller. This is a fact. He may be the best damn storyteller these parts or anyone's parts had ever seen or heard. Resole's stories encompassed all stories, they went hither and yon, they yinned and yanged, they yoyoed out to the end of the line and snapped back like a ricocheted comet. They were the discontinuation and the inauguration, amen, and the circle in a circle was maybe born in them and reiterated endlessly since, but that is just the warp and woof and the substance is what I'm gonna tell you now.

The story was only one story.

The story Resole told was the story of his life, his own precious life. It was the story of Beale Street. No one knows when he started telling it, along about his teen years near as anyone can figure but that is just mathematics and of no real interest. Resole told the story of his own life and he told it in such detail the telling took as long as the living and so you had to attend to the minutest thing, such is the life of every man, such are we all.

Believe it or don't.

Resole told about the schooling, about the raising, about the first stirrings in his primordials. He told about eating and singing and whispering and sleeping (though he slept when telling of the sleeping as you can imagine) and the playing and the shitting and the laughing and the crying and the masturbating and the bathing and every sigh and hiccup and blink and every time he changed the part in his hair. He told the waking in the morning, breakfast, newspaper, coffee, shave, perambulation, lunch, nap, telephoning, television, visits, dinner, the long liquid hours between repast and slumber, the silvery evenings, as slippery as memory, as powerful. He told the dreams and the disappointments and the hurt and the seven sins and the lies and the pride

and he told the love. He told it with an honesty of Biblical
proportions, a fury that holds men in its sway, a supranatural
thing.

The telling took as long as the living. Resole told the
story endlessly, rain or shine. One day he was there and the
telling had begun and it was a force of nature, or it was the
devil as some said, but it was as real as the rain and sun, as
tireless as the stars.

By the time of this here story Resole had already
passed the part of his life where the telling began and by now,
as we know, he was telling about the telling and his audiences
had dwindled and interest had waned but Resole McRey was
still a singularity and the wonder of him was undiminished.
Some people came back to hear tell about the parts where
they first appeared to listen, lo these many years ago, the
telling of the telling including all who listened, as must be.

The telling took as long as the living.

Some say Resole was the illegitimate offspring of a
furtive coupling between a once respectable white doctor
and a young tenebrous conjurewoman, years ago in the dim
twilight of the world, in the days before the music died. It
was hard to tell from Resole's hue just exactly what race
he was (human for sure, yes) due to the weathering of his
exterior. He may have indeed been a half-breed, who knows?

Some say Butterfly McQueen didn't even win the
Oscar, that she died prizeless, bereft. So there you go.

And Resole stood the same damn spot on Beale
Street every day of his life, as constant as the blues, as solid a
spectacle as the statue of Mr. Handy itself. *Mirabile dictu.* It's
said he was there in the beginning but we folks with more
sober inclinations understand that Resole McRey came from
somewhere and when he had gone he went back there, like the
tides maybe, like Brigadoon. Resole was the world's foremost
storyteller because Resole was the story himself.

Now rightly here is not the place to relate the story Resole told, the story of Resole. (Though the story necessarily encompassed many from here about.) His life is not yet transcribed and maybe never will be. I ain't the man to do it. And I've got other fish to fry.

This is the story of Butterfly McQueen's Oscar.

As I said.

Butterfly McQueen & the Angels of Beale Street

Now, Butterfly McQueen you all know and she doesn't figure prominently or at all in the proceedings, except in the form of a piece of her property which she reported missing and has been one of the foremost mysteries in the cockeyed annals of tinsel-town history, where that thing done gone. Anyway.

The Oscar itself, where did it go? Who spirited it away, and how, children, most pressing of all, did it end up in Mort Smalley's pawn shop on Beale Street in the year in which this story proceedeth. How indeed.

So, Ms. McQueen you know, and we mentioned Mort Smalley, but it was his daughters, his mirror-image daughters, Valerie and Vivian, who we wish to know better, yes. The witchy pale white twins with the radiance of their blond manes the subject of many county's worth of adoration and admiration. The gorgeous twins who were never apart, Siamese at the souls it's said, the opposite of Superman and Mr. Kent, one person in two bodies, people, those twins.

And it was the twins, the big-hearted twins, the ones who were always bringing in hurt bugs and stray dogs, who befriended the ragman, Freeman Blemish. They found him one afternoon on the east end of the street, bent like a kindergartener over a square of sidewalk, drawing circles with a stub of chalk. They stood over him reverently watching his intensity with an intensity of their own, as he drew loop after loop, circles within circles, his chalk diminishing like ice cream, seemingly eternal though, until it seemed the shaggy ragman was drawing with only a memory of chalk, the circles pulled from the air.

Finally he looked up, squinting, at the magnificent twins with the bright summer sun behind them, their shapely shapes rising from the earth like plantlife, their aforementioned aureoles of hair refracting light like cornsilk, and in short, Freeman Blemish thought he was experiencing a visitation. Yes, he thought angels stood before him and he was sore afraid.

"Sorry to disturb you," Valerie tinkled.

"Yes, sorry," Vivian echoed.

"Your circles are quite extraordinary," Valerie said.

"Would you like us to get you some more chalk?"

Freeman just squinted. The angels could speak.

"My name is Valerie and this is my sister Vivian."

Freeman's brain, missing links, connected that there were indeed two beings present, cut from the same supernal raiment. The angels stooped and their faces, though he was resistant to looking directly into them, came perilously close to his. They spoke again, or one of them did.

"Would you like some lunch?"

"Urg," Freeman managed. He was, as always, starved.

"Um, can we buy you a sandwich? Or would you like to come to our house for some of our father's Dogpatch Stew?"

And so the sisters led the befuddled ragman to their humble abode and began a friendship which took the three of them right into the middle of this story.

THE STORYTELLER'S FANS

Meanwhile the storyteller's story went on and on. A small lunchtime crowd normally attended, sandwiches in hand, dripping condiments like Jackson Pollock inspiration. A polite burble of commentary and applause awarded every pause, though most pauses were not breaks in the narrative flow but silences for emphasis, silences where there were silences in the history which was being unfolded. Wind in the interstices.

Of course, the bighearted twins loved Resole McRey. Often it was they who furnished him with meals and a warm place to lay his head (their nearby domicile, the aptly named *Betelgeuse*). They were his most faithful, his beloved devotees. Sometimes, and this is to go no further for there are minds out there still in their reptilian selfishness, small and unloving, sometimes the girls took care of Resole's other needs. It was the least they could do they figured, small recompense for the lifetimes of pleasure the indefatigable griot provided. But, at night, in the stillness of Beale Street penumbra, the lovely freemartins took Resole's chooza out of his attrited trousers and let it feel the fresh evening air and the nunlike ministrations of their silken palms. And, the beauty of it is, they never interrupted the story; with profound respect they waited for a period of untelling. Some say there is a small spot in the murky shadowed soil on Beale Street where Resole's seed has been gathering these many years and it will be there, on that spot of immaculate ejaculate, that something miraculous is predestined to occur. This is magical speculation, sure, we file it away as such.

A PORNOGRAPHIC OUTING

Ok, the statuette. It sat at the back of a back shelf at Smalley's Pawn Shop, burnished with age and outside of memory. No one knows how it got there, gypsies some conjecture, sold so long ago not even timeless Mort Smalley remembers from whence it came. Just one more knickknack in an emporium of knicked knickknacks, the jammed but unjammy pawn shop, where wares move as if with the winds, coming from there to here, from far away to near at hand, and soon gone again, the transport of the traffic of trade. The trade winds.

And then one day it had to come out. Old Mr. Smalley happened upon it searching for a beatup triton he knew was there somewhere, just what a peculiar, barbate gentleman was asking for. Mort pulled out the statuette with a short snort, set it aside and produced from the shadows a rusty trowel, turning sheepishly with it in his outstretched hand.

"Thank you, no," the elegant dandy pronounced, spinning on his heels and exiting.

But now Mort Smalley had had his attention drawn away and he hefted the Oscar in his gnarly old hand and brought it back to the counter with him. He was polishing it when his daughters popped in from the luminous Gehenna of the outdoor world.

"What's that, Pop?" Valerie asked, pulling a yellow Tootsie Roll sucker from her perfect mouth.

Vivian just smiled brightly, her tongue rolling around its own pineapple pop.

"Dunno, girls, found it on a back shelf. Methinks it's some kind of Greek thing. You know, classy. I'm thinking I can shine her up and ask a pretty penny, sell it to one of those tasteful East Memphis dopes," their industrious father answered.

"Sounds good, Father Mine," Valerie said.

Vivian bit down on her sweet mouthful with an abrupt crack.

"What are you two minks up to on this hellishly hot day?" their father asked them as the small statuette began to glow under his manipulation.

"We just took Resole his lunch and now we're thinking about going to the movies," one of the twins said.

"Unless you need us to help you," the other added hastily.

"Nah, nah. You two take the day off. Go see the Pola Negri thing. God I love that Pola Negri."

"Right, Pops," Valerie said, bussing her busy father quickly on his stubbly cheek.

And they blew out the door.

They weren't going to see Pola Negri--hell, they didn't even know who Pola Negri was. No, they were going to the Adult House that had just opened a few blocks over. They had been planning it for weeks, ever since they heard about its opening. Curiosity ran in them like bug juice. One of the musicians told them they showed people in full glorious nakedness, doing gloriously naked things. They couldn't even imagine it.

LOVE: A CRIME

So, we know where the Academy Awards statuette resides at this point. And the twins, the comely twins, are warm and snug in the unrenovated, threadbare theatre seats at Al's Adult Cinema on the corner of Third and Madison, watching a large-boned Swedish actress go down on the love muscle of a flat-bellied hustler and drug addict on the fireplace-sized off-white screen. They are happy. And Resole is tale-spinning, what else.

Freeman Blemish enters, stage right. He is loopy and weatherworn; he smells of canned fish. He squints at the heartless Southern sun. He is waving one loose-jointed arm wildly at the sky and he has one crooked appendage dug down deep in his bemired clothing fiddling with his own controls. Freeman is lost, Freeman is alien. Freeman is in love.

He makes his way across Beale and locates the door to the old man's pawn shop, knowing the way, memorizing the way. Freeman is looking for the angels, the seraphic Siamese. He wants to drown in their cupboard love.

Above his head a small tintinnabulation announces his arrival, the sound of Terpsichore tuning up. The old man at the counter has his back to the door and he turns slowly like in a dream--it is a dream, a dream Freeman has had somewhere in his forgotten past.

"Hello, Ragman," the wizened monger pronounces.

Freeman stands in the doorway with the sun streaming around him, confounded, composed of glim and dust mote. He is protean. He speaks.

"Love," he says.

"What is it, Freeman? What brings you here?"

The ragman looks wildly around the shop. They are here. He must get past the gatekeeper first. Task number one.

Freeman stalks forward, carried on air. He is in one place and then he is in another. He reaches a hand out (the one from inside his garments) and it hangs in the heightened atmosphere like a sword. It is waiting for the completion of a transmission.

It hangs like a scimitar, like justice.

The hand moves falteringly, sluggishly. It starts for the half-glasses suspended on the face before it, turns slightly, adjusts. It touches, lightly at first, the gleaming tip of a small, golden human being. It runs along the crown of its small head.

He likes the gentle curve of its pate. It talks to him; it belongs to him.

And then, swift as justice, the hand closes around that head, lifts and strikes. The old man falls. Slowly, like a jerky silent film, Mort Smalley falls. Freeman looks closely at the figure in his grasp, now touched at the tip with a magical drop of blood, which slides down the statue's face, a face reflecting Freeman's own, as if in a circus mirror, so that the sanguinolent drop, on its enchanted voyage, appears to be on Freeman's distorted visage. Freeman is hurt. He turns and runs, the twins forgotten now--what had he come for? his heart hurts, he is going to be sick--grasping the trophy like a talisman, out into the sun, straight into the sun.

SOME HARSH REALITIES

Who knew there would be blood spilt in the story? There is always blood spilt.

Who knew there would be sex, there would be the agitated congress of lubricated humans? There is always the lubricated congress of agitated humans.

Who knew the story had no destination? There is never a destination.

Who knew no one knew? No one, children, ever knows.

GHOSTS AND HISTORY SONGS

Did the shopkeeper die? Are our beautiful twins orphaned, cast on parentless shores?

Sorry to say, yes.

Mortimer Smalley was inearthed in Elmwood Cemetery, far from the Confederacy but near some heroes of Yellow Fever, on a cool, sunny day, with many in attendance. The twins read a section from Resole's tale (since, we understand, Resole could not be present) which was a particular favorite of their father's, a section about the flood on Beale and the Jewish writer who, in dreams, walked the newborn shores and remembered it all to recreate it later in Biblical prose, for all time, for all time.

Many of the aged dancers and entertainers from the defunct clubs came to pay respects. An old man sang an epicedium about Mississippi (Goddamn) and one of the dancers swayed slightly, her arthritic hips deep in recollection.

A wake came after, a wake in the wake of the blistering, Southern deader, the procession leading down Old Beale, past the scene of the murder, closed to business now forever, ghosts skittering into the gutters as the music went by, singing echoing from the heavens, songs about the history. History songs. Mort Smalley laid to rest.

SOMEONE WAS HURT

And the murderer, skulking in doorways, living in shadows, barely aware of his own guilt, but knowing he had done *something*, some harm, somewhere. Someone was hurt, hurt bad. That was what the keening meant. He huddled under old papers, yellowed with forgotten news. Freeman Blemish was trying to make himself smaller, trying to shrink like a werewolf, trying to disappear. The sunset found him cold and scrawny, a part of the street's debris, waiting for the final horn, waiting for the story to come back around.

LEONARD GUNSHY

Leonard Gunshy (pronounced gun' shee) had worked the Beale beat for most of his adult life. He was a tired cop and, for the most part, could care less. He could care less about prostitution, illegal gambling, illegal booze, knife fights, murder. Let them kill each other, he could care less. He'd seen it all, he'd lost two wives to divorce and half of his scrotum to a gunshot wound. He was drifting toward retirement like a rudderless craft.

He could care less, even about his own retirement.

But, dammit, Mort Smalley had been a friend, a lifelong friend. He decided after witnessing that moving procession down Beale that he cared enough to try and find the scoundrel who had beaten his friend to death with a blunt object. And to find the blunt object. Leonard Gunshy decided he was on the case. He was pulling out his dusty, trusty murder bag.

Also, adherents, Leonard Gunshy was in love with the twins.

LOVE AGAIN

The twins survived the loss of their second and last parent with the kind of resilience they have been noted for--part independent fire and part *joie de vivre*, a *joie de vivre* as intense as a delta rainstorm. They were voracious about life, even in the face of death and, it wasn't long after the untimely demise of their poor old progenitor, they were fixtures on the street once again, here feeding the shifting faces of homeless vagabonds, there administering definitive blowjobs to the

sturdy corey of the storied Resole McRey. Resole for his
part, profoundly chagrined at the loss of Mort Smalley, was
deepening the texture, the weave, the subtext of his telling,
casting it in a melancholy framework, keening it into the
sunny heavens and into the dusky twilight, in honor of a fine
man, whose daughters, well, were his sole delight.

And the bedraggled inspector spent many an afternoon
and evening on the corners of Beale Street, watching the
beautiful twins go about their business, making notes about
them, studying their every movement with a dedication
previously uncelebrated in the twisted annals of human heart
strings, all under the guise of digging into the case. He was
having a hard time getting back on track after years of ennui.
He was seriously sidetracked.

THE PROBLEM OF FREEMAN

Meanwhile, though perhaps not at the same time as
any of the action related above, Freeman Blemish had taken
up semi-permanent residence in a culvert north of downtown,
huddled under a mixture of cardboard and Styrofoam packing
material, cuddling to his chest his only connection to reality,
his lifeline. He held the bloodied Oscar like a baby holds its
blanket, like Thor held his hammer. It meant something to
him, something profound, maybe even tragic, but he could
not remember what. Long afternoons he stared at it, trying to
plumb its depths, to unlock the mystery of the statuette. He
crooned to it, questioned its sphinxic silence, rubbed it with
the alacrity of Aladdin. It answered not.

Freeman emerged from his culvert only to scrounge
food from dumpsters. He hurried on these gustatory missions
as if he had important business to attend to, or as if he were
expecting an important call back at the culvert. To be away
from home was anathema to him. What if he missed---what?
He couldn't say. But there was something imminent awaiting
him and it involved that mysterious statue, his salvation and
damnation both.

BACK TO BETELGEUSE

"Hello, Inspector," Valerie tinkled, but it could just as well have been Vivian.

"Ladies," Leonard Gunshy said, tipping an imaginary hat, awkwardly. He had abandoned his furtive skulking on corners for the forthright approach of talking directly to the young women. But it was like looking into the sun for him and he squinted and vellicated and shifted under his oversize coat and looked altogether moonstruck.

"What news brings you, our wise Inspector?" V or V tittered.

"Please call me Leonard," the Inspector said. No one had ever called him Leonard, not, that is since seventh grade, when Mrs. Parrish called him that right before she seduced him.

"Leonard," the twins said, in ignescent unison.

"I have no news, Ladies. I am doing a pitiful job. I admit, I am as lost as Atlantis. I have no leads."

"What have you done so far?"

"Whom have you questioned?"

Leonard Gunshy looked at his beatup, unfashionable shoes. He shuffled. He took a deep breath.

He looked from beatific face to beatific face.

"So far, " he said, clearing his catarrh. "I have only followed the two of you."

The twins smiled.

Leonard Gunshy continued.

"I am sorry. I have become tangled in my own web. I have been following your every move for weeks."

"And what have you discovered, Leonard?" one of the twins said while the other stood with her cheek fat with her own plump tongue.

"I have seen many things," he said. "I have discovered two saints in our midst, two angels from heaven. Ladies, I have fallen in love."

Here Leonard Gunshy burst into embarrassing tears. They flowed down his cheap raincoat, over his cardboard belt, across his partly jammed fly, over his service revolver. They popped on the dusty leather of his shoes, making a sound like music from a Disney film. He wept for his own uncaring soul, for the loss of his friend Mort Smalley, for his dishonor in front of the two finest women he had ever known.

Of course, the twins took the cheerless policeman to bed in Betelgeuse, their home, and undressed him and bathed him and anointed him with their own sweet musks, cleaning him like a cat her kittens, and in the end, Leonard Gunshy emerged a new man, one committed to action, younger than yesterday, a rededicated constable.

The twins went about their business.

An Unholy Rain

One day it rained an unholy rain on Beale Street in this latter half of the story, a soaking as sour as death, as deadly as a dogdeep depression. It fell like a final curtain, and the street was dark at noon. It swept through the alleyways with demonic winds, howling up from perdition, a dybbuk rain, a succubae mizzle. And the outside world was barren of life, as if indeed the final day had arrived and all were chosen, a cleansing rain then, the waters of abstergence.

It was grey, lowering, Stygian.

The world was empty.

Empty except for one lone soul, one left to witness. The storyteller.

The storyteller, soaked to the bone, to the marrow, to his soul, never missed a lick. The water greased his taletelling machinery; the story took on a watery shine, a slicker, heavier value, a retted legend, wind-whipped and liquid-laden. And in the dim distance, shadowed with the screen of falling rain, outlined like a drawing of death, drawing nearer, came another lone figure, a vagarious pariah, moving inexorably toward Resole as if rolling on rusty wheels. There in the middle of Beale the confrontation grew more imminent second by second, and if there had been anyone to notarize they would have sworn that Resole moved also. But, no. He was as stationery as Old Man Schwab's and all the movement was towards him, as if he were the Pole.

It is open to speculation as to whether Resole McRey paused in his telling, or even if he was aware of the stranger coming toward him in the rain. The story went on. As steady as the rain. A rainstory.

But in the closing seconds of the newcomer's arrival, recognition spread in Resole like a virus. He knew the face which now materialized out of the dim. It was the face of the ragman, the face of Freeman Blemish.

Who stopped just a doorgap from the storyteller's personal space. And spoke.

"I killed him," Freeman Blemish said, his words overlapping an account of a grey, nondescript day from the seventies, a day when two foreigners went to the movies in downtown Memphis and saw a movie they didn't understand, and left holding hands. An uneventful day woven deep into the fabric of the narrative, told with relish and elevation.

Was there a pause in the story? Some say so, most say no. It is unknown whether Resole absorbed the confession, understood it for what it was. But he thought of the twins; he wished the twins were here with him.

"I killed him with this," Freeman said, brandishing a small gold human figure.

"I am vengeance, lost vengeance," he further articulated and his sense began to run out as if there were a hole in the bucket of his head. "I am Torn Asunder, the wicked one. I am Golf and Dinner. I am Whiskerweed. Love me for who I am. I am W-wisdom. I have been to the foul places and drunk there, Lord, Lord. I am the sleep at the end of the dream; I am the ed-edge of your emptiness. I am Infernal Beeeeeeswax. I am Need, Nod. Look upon me and be glad. I am Love, I am Love, I am. I am. I, I, I."

And he paused. The rain continued, clattering.

"I am the Storyteller."

And he threw his arms around Resole and Resole took him in his own arms and the rain and the story went on all around them and the street was deserted except for them and the world was deserted except for them and it went this way for a while until Freeman broke off and, without looking back, faltered away into the indistinct day.

A Message Arrives

Leonard Gunshy awoke from a dream about the twins and the sun was coming in like a second-story man and he shook his stubbly face to try and clear his head. Had he heard a dull noise, a muffled knock, or was that his dream, a heartbeat in his dream? He shuffled to his front door and, squinting like a mole-man, opened the door to the world.

He was blind for a long time and when he could finally see he wished he had remained blind. On his stoop was a small dead bird which had apparently flown into his door. A kamikaze bird.

And stuck in the rubberband of his newspaper, like a gun in a waistband, was a note, a soiled corner of paper, folded once. A kamikaze, messenger bird? But Leonard doubted the bird had taken the time to place the note underneath the rubberband. His reason was intact.

He picked up the news and unfolded the piece of paper, which felt like a much-circulated dollar bill, soft with handling.

There was a blue scrawl, cramped and shaky.

And it said:

Look for the small gold man.

There is much speculation as to who left the telltale. Evidence points to Resole McRey, but this would be an unprecedented form of communication from the man. Leonard Gunshy didn't join in the speculation. He took the note very seriously indeed and he could care less from whence it came. He was sure it was the break he had been waiting for.

After he had showered and dressed he put the message into his jacket pocket and went out with a purpose. He began asking around about the "small gold man." He checked with all his usual sources and they all thought he was mad, loopy, dippy.

A small gold man, Leonard pondered over his deli sandwich lunch. And after considerable pondering the ideation formed in his pondering that he maybe was searching for a piece of art, a sculpture, *a statuette.*

He renewed his questioning, formulating his inquiry around the search for a small gold statue. Still he came up empty.

It was at the end of the third day Leonard ended up at Betelguese, where he found the twins watching Jeopardy. He sat in an understuffed armchair and put his hand into the popcorn bowl.

"What is Valhalla?" the twins said.

"What is Valhalla?" the TV intoned.

"Who is Kaspar Hauser?" the twins said.

"Who is Kaspar Hauser?" the TV snapped back.

"What is 'Mississippi Lowdown Blues'?" the twins said with particular zest.

And again the echo came.

Leonard Gunshy wanted to contribute but the twins tied his tongue. And they were faster.

"What is Uruguay?" the anxious detective jumped in, startling the women, who grimaced sympathetically.

"What is Paraguay?" the TV admonished.

The twins reached over and patted Leonard on the knee. He sunk into humiliated suppression.

At the next commercial break Leonard emerged from his self-imposed exile and sighed as preface to speaking.

"I have a lead, ladies," he said.

"Ahh," they entwined.

"It is a curious lead, a puzzle in itself," and he gave a deprecating snort. "I believe, though, that if I can solve this riddle I can solve the larger one."

"We are intrigued," one of the duplicates said.

"What is this enigmatic clue, Leo?" the other said.

Leonard unfolded the wrinkled note and laid it out on the coffee table next to the popcorn bowl.

The twins leaned over and read the scribbled message.

They bobbed back up, concurrently.

"The Oscar," they said.

Some Things Become Clearer

Leonard Gunshy listened carefully as the twins explained how they had seen the statuette on the dusty, mingle-mangled shelves of their late father's pawn shop. With their usual prescience they glommed onto what it was but thought no further about it. After all, Smalley's Pawn

Shop was the final resting place of all manner of remarkable gewgaws and kickshaws. They had bowling pins, snorkels, a parachute, a pitchpipe, scrimshaw, a printer's brayer, a tatting shuttle. They had trusses, dentures, church keys, a pacemaker, a policeman's baton, an S-band steerable antenna from the lunar landing module. They had fanbelts, fan magazines and fans. They had a purser's pump, a piggy-stick, a Paddy Quick. Also, an oar, a bolo tie, a lorgnette, a pipe tool, a candle snuffer, an icing syringe, a branding iron, an allen wrench and the Pope's own toothbrush. They had a piece of the prototype cross. What was one Oscar more or less, they reasoned, amid all that accumulated abundance. There must be thousands of them, what with costume designers, cinematographers, sound effects nerds, and the special assistant grip's nephew eligible for one. So an Academy Award ended up in their pop's pawn shop. No big deal.

They could not have known that it once belonged to the exanimate star of *Gone With the Wind*, though they were of the few who believed she had received one, (history being malleable) along with her more famous dusky cohort, Mammy. They could not have known that its value increased because there were questions about its very existence. With every day it stayed missing another dollar was tacked onto its imagined assessment.

Leonard Gunshy accepted the explanation. He was giddy with gratitude and kissed both girls, impulsively, on their respective cheeks. He leapt into action and out the door.

It did not take him long to locate a bum who knew another bum who had seen another bum with an Oscar under his arm. The skinny was that he lived in a culvert on the Northern side of town. They pinpointed the current address of our befuddled antihero, Freeman Blemish.

Leonard closed in.

The Return of Freeman

The return of Freeman Blemish, coming as it does penultimately, will be seen here and elsewhere as some sort of crux. A machina of some sort, perhaps deus ex. But stories rise and fall, rise and fall, a sign curve, signifying not much, going on their way lonely as a cloud. We try to put order to them, whip them with the lash of our sense and try to pen them, herd them, tame them. They will comply, nodding along, for a while. For a while.

Then they can turn on their masters.

So the storyteller's story rambles and rumbles and moves like a river at floodstage, wandering like a plaintive shadow. His story, this one.

It is told: The return of Freeman Blemish came about this way:

The culvert was empty, deserted. Devoid of Blemish.

There was evidence of previous inhabitance, candy wrappers, Sprite cans, spilth and spatter, unmentionables. Leonard Gunshy was like a happy hound, an old dog out on the hunt again.

He learned that Blemish was haunting the Beale Street area again. He had several spottings of him, he had a description.

It was dusk and the tired but energized detective was sitting in Handy Park, humming blues tunes and letting his mind unwind. Some hundred yards or so away the storyteller droned, a musical background both cordant and dis.

As Cimmerian shade crept slowly over the street the twins appeared with dinner for Resole. Leonard imagined they would lead the griot into the shadows again and perform their genitive ablutions and he was happy about this as if he were witness to the rightness of things, to the natural patterns of a weary world. A third figure appeared from the East, forming an uneven quadrilateral with Resole, the Twins and Leonard Gunshy himself the reference points. This figure moved like a scarecrow come to life, as if he only lacked a brain. It careened, but slowly, crepitatingly.

It was Freeman Blemish, of course. But hold the suspense a moment longer--our heroes know this not.

Vivian and Valerie were unwrapping a meatball sandwich, unscrewing the top of a thermos (with a semi-nostalgic momentary passing thought as to the fate of thermos corks) full of Mountain Dew, and half-listening to the story of a cacodemon and his mate who used to work out of the backroom of Sweeney's a few years back selling homemade hooch. The storyteller, they stopped to muse, was in rare form.

The seemingly drunken tatterdemalion emerged from shadow to light. It was a cartoon of an arrival, the murderer out of Looney Tunes, East of Eden.

Leonard Gunshy got shakily to his feet.

Freeman Blemish stopped in the middle of the street and his head bobbed on the stem of his neck like a car ornament. He brought his slowly focusing eyes to rest on the slowly moving form of Leonard Gunshy. He thought he was the most beautiful man he had ever seen; he fell in love with Leonard Gunshy as quickly as a scalded cat goes through a back window. And, as quickly as he fell in love with him, he knew this: he had to destroy him.

Leonard Gunshy stood frozen in Handy Park, his hands raised in front of him, as if they were playing freeze tag. He stood in the shadow of W.C. Handy's statue and unconsciously mirrored him. The moment was fraught with world-turning drama. The smell of red sauce filled the air.

Vivian and Valerie squinted toward the end of the street, half-smiles stuck awkwardly on their divine faces. They were confused. They were in a story.

Freeman Blemish had both of his hoary hands deep in the pockets of his weather-worn overcoat. In one hand he clutched a grimy pistol he had recovered from a dumpster. In the other the Oscar. His misfiring grey matter worked on the problem of which to pull out. "A man destroys the thing he loves," he heard his inner voice mutter as if it were drunk and only half-interested. "A thing of beauty is a joy forever," again.

He hesitated. His shoulders made preliminary movements which signaled the appearance of one of his hands. He saw Mr. Handy's horn and wished for his hands to know something that intimately. Quickly, like a gunslinger, he pulled his left hand from his coat pocket.

Leonard Gunshy reacted with a lifetime's training. His service revolver whisked into the cool evening air swift as a thought. It barked once.

Vivian and Valerie both screamed. "No," they bansheed simultaneously, splitting the air, dislodging rooks and night-owls and bats. Resole McRey stopped talking.

Resole McRey stopped talking.

Freeman Blemish hit the ground hard. He fell like a pile of cans. Out of his filthy grasp the Oscar flew, skittering along the pavement like a puck.

Leonard Gunshy dropped to his knees and burst into tears. The flying animals circled once, twice and re-lighted.

The End of Story, Story Continues

Time passed and people came back to Beale Street. People came back to hear Resole McRey. Word got out again, word perseverated.

The crowds grew, sluggishly at first, like the bleeding of one season into another. Resole became popular again, inexplicably perhaps, why now, why ever? Time passed and the story changed and the people in the crowd recognized the names in the story and once again they became part of it and Resole's fame spread like a whore's legs, pardon me.

"It isn't all skittles and beer," as Leonard Gunshy used to say.

Resole told the legend of Butterfly McQueen's Oscar.

Eventually Resole McRey moved on, like legend, children, gone but to our recollection. But it was not the death of Freeman Blemish which occasioned the change, know that.

Because first the people came back to Beale.

People came back to Beale to hear about the past, about the shop owner felled by a dead Negro actress's disinherited and once-denied Academy Award, to hear about the twins who visited briefly from Zion, about the bravery of a grizzled police veteran, about the swiftness of justice, and the unreliability of renown.

The Oscar went back to the pawn shop's shelves. The pawn shop became a small museum. Valerie and Vivian moved up North--you've heard of them. Leonard Gunshy retired, remarried, died unhappy. Freeman Blemish was buried in Elmwood Cemetery--the twins saw to that--near Mort Smalley. Some forgiveness conquered death.

Resole McRey told on and on, his name written down nowhere, the story unfolding around him like heavenly robes, uncoiling like revelation.

TWO FROM THE BLUES PLAYERS TRADING CARDS
(COLLECT ALL 1,027)

Sweet Annie Divine

Sweet Annie Divine (1925-1976). Born Rooster, Arkansas, Annie May Auspex. Also known as The Duchess. Dropped out of school at the age of 13 to work her parents' cotton fields. Started singing professionally at 16 in juke joints in Arkansas, Mississippi and Tennessee. Toured with Jimmy Reed for a while, sang with Styx Ygg's BamBam Five on Beale Street in the forties. Fronted her own band, The Moxie Seven (or Eight depending on the night), which included Hillbilly Thomas and Sweetie Sykes and they had a mid-major hit with "Stephen Daedalus's Blues" in 1948. Recorded "Chicken Finger Blues," "Write Em Right," "Saint Ursula Goes Down for the Third Time," and her signature tune "Mississippi Lowdown Blues" for the Lightning Label. She is credited with the composition of only one standard, the rocking "Lemme Get Up First," later, of course, covered by The Rolling Stones. Her last record for a major label was a cover of Holmes and Howard's "Somebody's Been Using That Thing." Comparisons to Big Mama Thornton and Bessie Smith brought her a brief renaissance of interest in the restless sixties. She died of the drink in a Memphis boarding house, just hours after recording her last record, the plaintive and pain-filled "I'm a Drunk in a Memphis Boarding House." Alan Lomax has said of her, "She could have been one of the greats if not for the hooch."

Seven Finger Tucker

Seven Finger Tucker (1920--2000). Born Belial Alloys Tucker in Watered Down, Tennessee. Songwriter and slide guitar player, nicknamed "Seven Finger" after the devil took three of his fingers on a bet, so the story goes. Wrote for and worked with many of the greats, Charlie Patton, W.C. Handy, Willie Dixon, Little Walter, Johnny Shines and Bumble Bee Slim. Tucker was a studio musician at Chess from 1940 to 1951, playing on many of their greatest releases, often uncredited. Wrote the standards, "The Gal Messed Me Up, She Messed Me Up Good," "Her Ass Moves I Moan," "Wrinkle Here Wrinkle There," "Quarrel & Quandary Blues" and "They Bribe the Lazy Quadling." Moved to Memphis in the fifties and stayed there until his death, playing anywhere he was asked, sometimes just for the price of a meal. In 1978 he became a regular performer at Club Royale on Beale and earned something of a reputation as a ladies' man. He sang often with Furry Lewis at the Mid-South Fair, at church revivals and other incongruous gigs. In 1998 he received a Handy Award for Lifetime Achievement. He also wrote "Partridge's Dictionary of Slang and Unconventional English Blues" for Willie Nelson's Milk Cow Blues cd and which Nanci Griffith included on her third collection of covers, "Last Voices in Other Rooms, Including the Guest House Out Back." Seven Finger Tucker invented his own idiosyncratic slide style, which can be heard on cds from artists as wide ranging as Spiritualized, B. B. King and Julio Iglesias. He died of complications from cosmetic surgery. When asked by Living Blues Magazine in 1999 the source of his longevity and good health he said, "Ex-lax and the blues."

"Mississippi Lowdown Blues:"
A Song

lyrics by Seth Adamson
music by Ava Joe

Mississippi Lowdown Blues

I live in a apartment

I ain't worked in sixteen year

How'm I gonna wander

If I can't get outa here?

I gots a wife, I gots a fam'ly

A dog and a cat

Hows I supposed to feel

With somethin like that?

I got the lowdown blues

That's why I sing this song

I got the Mississippi lowdown blues

How long, Lord, how long?

I gots the man down on the corner

I gots the man at the bank

I gots the man with the police siren

Gonna throw me in the tank

I gots me four ugly women

They givin me fits

I gots two ugly sisters

With sco-li-o-sis

Chorus

My baby took my money

Leastwise all I had

She took it down to Beale Street

She ain't never comin back.

Now the world is made a pyrite

Least that's what they say

Gonna live till I'm a dead man

In New Erusalemjay

I got the lowdown blues

That's why I sing this song

I got the Mississippi lowdown blues

How long, Lord, Oh how long?

I got the Mississippi lowdown blues

There ain't nothing really wrong.

(BLUES SHUFFLE) MISSISSIPPI LOWDOWN BLUES

I LIVE IN AN APARTMENT I AIN'T WORKED IN SIXTEEN
YEAR
HOW'M I GONNA WANDER IF I CAN'T GET OUTTA
HERE GOTS ME
A WIFE GOTS ME A FAMILY A DOG AND A CAT
HOW'S I SUPPOSED TO FEEL WITH SOMETHIN' LIKE THAT? I GOT THE
LOWDOWN BLUES THAT'S WHY I SING THIS
SONG. I GOT THE
MISSISSIPPI LOWDOWN BLUES HOW LONG LORD, HOW
LONG?

Conjuration: A Fabliau

 *a song is anything that can walk by itself."*

Bob Dylan

In the days when magic was plentiful and sacred (rather than the vice versa we know today) there lived near Beale Street in Memphis a man of extraordinary powers name of Beaureguard Rawhead. He was, as a conjureman, quite remarkable, but he wanted to be something else. He wanted to be a songwriter.

He had seen W.C. Handy as a youth and he had been thunderstruck. Suddenly all his magic was as if nullified. He wanted to conjure something as powerful, as universal as "St. Louis Blues," or "Mister Crump."

And as he grew older, and his fame as a powerful magicman grew, the need to produce just one memorable song grew, too, until it was an authoritative obsession. So, when the bluesman, Tiny Red, came to see Beaureguard about some business, he saw the chance for a right proper tit for tat.

Tiny Red was from Arkansaw by way of New Orleans by way of the Orient, which is to say Tiny was a grabbag of musical inventiveness. You know him best for "Silver Dollar Pantleg Blues" and "A Frothing of Delight" and for inventing the phrase "Your world." But, in his day, Tiny was as hot as they come, as big as Big Bill. In his tiny way, of course.

Tiny came to Memphis that fateful fall to scout up some talent for a travellin gig he was offered on the European continent. Most specifically he needed a second guitar and he heard tell of a Memphis bar rat name of Pete Holder played like the murmur of dreaming brooks. This was the word that he got.

He spent about a month on Beale scouting talent but he wasn't having any luck finding the elusive Mr. Holder. Some said they had just seen him, some said no he was in California. Some nights he was told he had just missed him. He's working at BingoBango, he was told, but no, when he got there he hadn't played there since last week.

But Tiny hadn't come to see Beaureguard Rawhead for no guitar player, no, naturally he came to see the conjureman for an affair of the heart. Seems Tiny had a major heartdeep crush on a dancer at one of the clubs, a woman with a rear like a Buick 6, comely like a pine bridge. Named Callie.

Tiny came, like so many before him, for a philter. He disbelieved in his own charm, in his personal ability to woo so fine a female, so he sought a charm outside of normal human makeup. A love potion.

Tiny knocked tentatively on Beauregard's tinplated door, anxious for thaumaturgy.

"Who?" Beau growled.

"Tiny Red Montgomery," Tiny swallowed. "From Arkansaw."

"Don't know ye," the answer.

"I need some help, sir."

"All God's children do."

"I was told you were the man to see bout this," Tiny said, a little bolder.

"Who said that?"

"Squiggly Robbins, for one. Bob Dobolina. Skincat Resin. All told."

"You music man?" Beau asked with a twinkle.

"That's right."

"Bluesman."

"Yea. Yessir."

"You are welcome."

Tiny ducked entering the cramped quarters, dark as time. There was a jumble of material everywhere, tables piled with books and manuscripts, papers on top of an old upright piano, every surface obscured by knickknacks and gewgaws, objects seemingly floating in the air. One stooped, sidestepped, bent and shuffled to see the munificent wizard of Beale.

Who sat grinning in a burnished chair, a smile like a keyboard.

"Sit, sit," the old man gestured vaguely.

Tiny carefully pushed aside some papers and settled on an upturned crate.

The magicman fixed him with a milky eye.

"You know W.C. Handy?" he asked quickly.

Tiny hesitated. Know his music or know the man, he wondered. He had actually met the great man once in Montgomery, Alabama, in a dark club, shook his hand, even. This seemed like some kind of test.

"I play his supernal music in my act," he brought out, finally.

"Ahhh," Beau said. "I believe we can do some transacting."

The deal Beauregard Rawhead laid out for the bluesman was simple but onerous. When he found out Tiny wanted a love potion (he coulda guessed, it was his main business) he allowed as to how he could grant him his every romantic wish in exchange for something a little less tangible. He wanted to be taught how to write a song.

Tiny rubbed his hand across his face, leaned back, leaned forward again. He blew out a bit of sour wind.

"I dunno," he began.

"No deal then."

"Mr. Rawhead, writin songs. I dunno, it can't be taught."

"You learned."

"No sir, I was born writin songs."

"Naw," Beau said and he grinned like a warden.

Tiny knew he was gonna agree to this, he just wanted the disclaimers up front.

"I can try it, sir. I can sure try it."

"Thas all I'm asking, " Beauregard said, standing up.

Tiny rose too. The two men shook hands. They agreed to start that very evening.

That evening the sunset in Memphis was red like the blood of Abraham, the river sucking up that color like a lamia, like a mother dog. There was an eeriness in the air, a tone underneath the everyday, like a buzz in the distance, like cicadas from another world.

Tiny showed up on time, as the bright, white day was giving way to vespertine purples. The old conjureman was eager to get started; he had cleared a space around his piano, like one might clear the ground to build a fire, or make a sacrifice.

Under his arm Tiny carried a sheaf of papers in a beatup folder, his songs. He spread those out on the piano keys and Beaureguard glanced at them perfunctorily.

"Don' need these," he said.

Tiny stared at him a second.

"Mr. Rawhead, lemme get started. You need to learn the musical notation. This the language of the music, the alphabet. Can't build no song without this."

"Don't want to build no song. Wan to..." and he stopped, seemingly to change his tack. "Awright. I see. Teach me this," he said, tapping the sheets.

They spent most of that evening going over basic notes and melodies, Tiny using the out-of-tune piano to demonstrate the sound beneath the symbol.

It was 2 a.m. when he put his long arms above his head and stretched himself with a crackling of bones.

"That's about it for tonight, I guess."

"Don't know how to write no song, yet," said the old man petulantly.

"Takes some time, sir."

"Awright, awright."

A week passed this way. Small advances, stubborn setbacks. The two men at loggerheads, butting them.

After two weeks the men were more cordial, whiskey between them, good talk. They spoke of love, sex, the river. A bond formed like electricity and the lessons took on a new compeerage.

And progress was made in the manufacture of a song.

Who woulda believed it? Beau began to see the warp and woof of music, began to comprehend its sortilege, its special fluidity. Music spoke to him in his dreams and waking he spoke back. He began to hum around the house, tunes coming in like broken radio waves, indistinct at first, scattered. Gradually a cohesion commenced like his newfound fraternity with Tiny, some kind of coming together.

Secretly at first he began to cobble together a few lines, a phrase or two with accompanying melody. A song was perceived through the dim, a strain appearing in the murk. Beaureguard in private seclusion was writing a song, unsure about revealing it to his master, the man who gave him music.

For his part Tiny suspected the old man was onto something. A new lilt to his conversation emerged, a new lightness to his banter. And in his muddy eyes blue stars danced sometimes, tiny shots like sparks off an anvil. Magic commencing.

The party to celebrate the partnership of Tiny Red and his new guitar player (it was Andy Love due to the mysterious fact that Pete Holder never materialized) was held at the Club BingoBango on a mild Friday night in October. Word spread that there was to be an all night jam and a number of the great and near-great and never-to-be-great attended. At one sweat-retted point in the proceedings, there on the same modest stage sat in Mississippi Red, Alexander Jimspake, Styx Quetzelcoatl, Big Bill Broonzy, The Lonely Dog, Robert Jung, Jimmy the Snake, Ed Alexander, Pudding Puddinski the chanteuse, Roman Rebus, John Kills-Her (the Native American harp player), Squeaky Joint, Tuff Green, the Shawcross Brothers, Skeets Cameron and the Duchess herself. It was a callathump, a shivaree. A bombast. And it was the first time, historically speaking, that the word "bluesfest" had been used. It was coined that night. Write it down.

Long after midnight, the conversation a murmur of ghosts and drinking men, the air fuliginous, almost unremarked Beaureguard Rawhead slipped in through the back door. On the stage Styx and Peep-eye Harper were weaving a sleepy rondo, which sounded a little like "Back'em up Blues in D." Everyone was sorta half there and half woolgathering.

Beaureguard slid up to the stage and took a seat at the 88s and looked at them with a kind of wonder and amusement and the other two musicians hesitated and the crowd sort of hummed and burbled and there was a few seconds of dusty silence.

Beaureguard touched the first key with his left hand pointer and some other keys followed and before anyone could quite assemble their thoughts he started singing softly, almost to himself at first. The words were incomprehensible initially then took form and poured forth, Beaureguard finding a voice as thick as annihilation, as sinuous as ice. Tiny rose slowly from his seat in the middle of the dim and din and hung there like a suspended orb. It was a minor miracle. It was better than he thought possible. The conjureman had a voice, a reason to sing.

And it was on that night that the now standard number, "Saprophytic Blues" was born.

Beaureguard had a minor singing and songwriting career, nothing matching the magic of that firstborn number (though The Latin Students had a minor hit with one of his songs, "They Bribe the Lazy Quadling" in the early fifties). His soul was at peace, however.

The other side of the bargain was, surprisingly, not as successfully achieved, even to making Beaureguard Rawhead cry out to his dark gods, "What good am I who cannot make the smallest world over?"

It wasn't that he gave Tiny Red a faulty philter, a no-motion potion. The elixir worked, oh yes.

Tiny took the small crystal bottle home with him and sprinkled it on his hairbrush as instructed. He lit the brush and it burned with a steady purple flame with a tiny red center like the back of a black widow as expected. But he never again saw Callie Pidgeon, the woman he had so set his heart upon winning.

He went to the strip club to see her perform and was told she had disappeared. Poof, like a thought.

His heart ached and he knew an emptiness hitherto undiscovered, and he spent some lonely nights wandering Beale, in a trance-like funk.

He forgave the old conjureman, attaching no blame to the failure of the contract. He was sad but not bitter.

"I failed you, boy. I need to make it up to you," Beaureguard said, hangdoggedly.

"It's okay, Beau. I'm okay."

"Man needs love, Tiny."

"It'll come."

"Let's go get us some Zombi Killers, drink ourselves outa the blues. What say?"

"I don' know, Beau. I don't feel right out on the street anymore. Something's wrong."

"What wrong?"

"Weirdness. Collywobbles. Somebody following me."

"Who do that?"

Tiny Red looked up at his friend. Tiny's eyes were deep sad, red-rimmed.

"Old woman. I look up. She everywhere I go. I dunno, she's okay, I guess. Kinda pretty. But, I don' need nobody following me, you follow?"

"Right."

The two men sat in stony silence for a few moments, the love between them like a cat. The air was tinny, faraway music somewhere.

"I get rid of that woman," Beaureguard spoke. "I make you a potion. By the way, Brother, I saw Pete Holder today."

BEALE STREET: AN ODE
by Vivian Smalley

It's the same ole story told
about us
about the old days
days as beleaguered as Old Sol himself.

How the Sun set specially
kindly on a little street of blue,
how it lingered over the river
and spread its benevolence

like a music, son, far
and then wide. It's a story
about the past when
there was no future, about

the man who sang a song

about himself, maybe,

a song which went on into the red

night and survived him.

And here at this end of the

street a woman sells herself

and over here a little piece

of rib, say, Adam's, say

it all together. I was the one

sang the song, I was the one

played those blues, mister,

call me Epiphany, son, call me Jack,

call me right before the note

ends, like a birdsong hung

in the breeze. Call me

History, son, Misery,

daughter, call me Beale Street.

Real Beale:
A Tragicomedy and a Play

Edward "Jolly" Newbacon found high school a trying experience. He had few friends, no desire to learn, no athletic skills and only a modicum of good looks.

Actually, in certain lights, he resembled the actor Anthony Perkins and this was good and bad, as you can imagine. And, actually, he had one good friend, Katy Schoemaker, who was as near a girlfriend as Edward had ever had. And, furthermore, *actually*, he did have a desire for new knowledge in some particular areas of study.

Edward "Jolly" Newbacon was dabbling in the occult.

It began when he saw a show on Discovery about Elizabethan England and heard the story about the court occultist, John Dee. Jolly became fascinated with Dee and became convinced he could follow Dee's lines of inquiry and-- and this was his target--conjure an angel.

From a midtown bookstore he acquired some of Dee's own writings and a few new books about him. The clerk in the store sold him the material with a wry grin.

"John Dee, eh?" he asked.

"Yes," Jolly allowed. "Know about him?"

"A little," the clerk followed.

"Project for school," Jolly said as he turned on his heel and scuttled out the door.

And, it was some coincidence, if we believe in coincidence, when the following week, while ambling desultorily through an antique mall's wending rows of "junque" with Katy, he came across the crystal ball.

It was lying in amongst some World War II memorabilia in a dusty cardboard box. A ray of light glinted off its clear, orbiculate surface, attracting Jolly's attention, drawing him in like a fish. Hooked, he dropped his hand into the rubble, pushing aside a bayonet, some tarnished medals, a dented canteen, and pulling it up into the air as if he had just liberated Excalibur.

"Katydid," he called exuberantly.

She was a couple of rows away, fingering old stage costumes.

"Jesus, Jolly, don't yell," she said, finding him.

"It's Dee's ball, look," he expostulated.

"Left or right," she drawled.

But Jolly was rapt, immune to sarcasm. He hurried toward the checkout desk, digging in his pockets for crumpled bills and change.

"How much?" he practically spat.

"Lemme see," the grizzled female proprietor said around a moist, brown cigarette, taking the glass ball from his hand.

"Hmm," she said, studying it like a gypsy. "Pretty old."

"It might be John Dee's," Jolly said, unused to the methods of moneychangers, the interlingua of the haggle.

"John D. Rockefeller, you say," she said, cash register bells tinging in her cranium. "Ten dollars," she pronounced finally.

"I've got six-sixty," Jolly said, throwing an imploring look back at Katy.

"I've got some money," she said, sighing, and laying her serving girl's crinoline and apron on the counter.

On the way home Jolly held the ball in his sweaty hands as if he thought it might dematerialize.

"Whatcha gonna do with that?" Katy asked, politely.

"Conjure an angel," he answered, flatly.

"Uh huh."

"My parents are going out of town next weekend. That's when I'll do it. That gives me scant time to purify myself and learn the proper incantations."

"Don't get too pure if your folks are going out of town," Katy said with her best leer. But it didn't even register. Jolly was off in fairyland.

At school Jolly had become a mediocre student after early years of great promise. During one phase of his academic career he had fancied himself a writer and published a few poems in the school literary journal, The Scribe. It was for this he was known, if he was known at all.

Mrs. Parrish, his English teacher, approached him fourth period.

"Can I have a word with you, Mr. Newbacon?" she inquired sweetly. It wasn't that she called her students by their last names generally; she just hated the moniker Jolly, especially for such a sullen student.

"Sure, Mrs. Parrish."

"There's a citywide writing competition sponsored by the Chamber of Commerce I thought you might be interested in," she said in one breath, after Jolly had seated himself.

"I'm, like, not really into writing as much," he mumbled.

"Now, you're our best writer, Mr. Newbacon," she twittered.

"Thank you, Mrs. Parrish. What kind of writing contest?"

"Well, it's for a one-act play, involving city history. I thought it might be right up your alley, what with your reading and all." She had no idea what she meant but the stab was closer to home than she realized.

"History," Jolly said, closing one eye. "I'll think about it."

"Ok, that's the spirit," she said with a dismissive smile. Young people made Mrs. Parrish nervous. No one knows why she wanted to be a teacher.

Jolly's parents were middle-aged suburbanites, like the parents of nine-tenths of the students of the county high school Jolly attended. It was a white-flight area of Memphis, which at this time in its history, was not a part of the city, and hence, its inhabitants, for the most part, felt not at all a part of the city's culture, tradition or political structure. The county's system was mostly white. The city's mostly black.

So it was no wonder Jolly had no connection to Memphis or its Chamber of Commerce or their boosterism. He could care less and he would not write for a city which disenfranchised him. Besides, he was no longer a writer, he was a magus.

During the grueling days leading up to his first grand experiment, Jolly put himself through a regime which would have made a religious flagellant proud. He drank no alcohol, ate no junk food, had no sex, not even with himself. He drank purified water from the jug his mother kept on the ironing board. He had contact with no one except his parents (necessarily) and Katy, and he barely acknowledged her.

One evening on the phone her exasperation boiled over.

"Jolly, cut this crap out, you're fucking pure enough," she huffed.

"I've only got two more days. Saturday night is a go."

"And I wanna *go* with you."

"Impossible."

"What, you're not even gonna see me this weekend?" she choked out.

"I can't, Katydid. What's with the proprietariness suddenly?"

She was caught. She loved him, what could she say?

"Oh. Well. I just thought, you know, you being alone and all. How many opportunities like that present themselves to teenagers? I'm tired of the car sex is all."

"Mm," Jolly said, noncommittally.

"I'm sorry, Jolly," Katy now said. "I'll leave you alone."

"Naw," Jolly relented. "You can, uh, come. But you gotta do what I tell you."

"Sure, Master. How about I wear that maid's costume I bought?"

"Yeah, yeah," Jolly said, already re-entering his dreamstate.

Saturday morning Jolly kissed his parents goodbye, his heart pounding. He felt ready. He felt strong and clean. He felt as pure as speechless infancy.

"Now, honey," his mother said, wiping her lipstick off his cheek with a stiff thumb. "Aunt Kecksie is just a phone call away. And you have the number where we're gonna be. We'll be back Sunday night."

"Yeah, Ma, I'll be all right."

As soon as he was alone he went straight to the books of incantations he had been studying and pored over them for most of the morning. Katy called once but he didn't even pick up and her voice on the answering machine sounded anxious and put-upon. If he had registered it clearly it would be like an axe-blade on a grinding stone, but he heard her not.

He ate nothing all day, running on nervous energy. As the afternoon stretched out he longed for the sun to set. He was ready and wanted only to begin. To let it all begin.

Katy arrived at six o'clock, a shy lasciviousness coloring her young innocence.

She bussed his cheek and breezed past him, throwing herself on the couch, one leg over its arm.

Jolly stood uncertainly in the doorway, staring at her as if he couldn't imagine how this stranger had wormed her way into his parent's house.

"Where?" she asked.

"Uh, my room," Jolly said, weakly.

"Great," Katy said, hopping up. She ran up the stairs and pushed into Jolly's bedroom.

When Jolly followed he found her standing next to the bed, his Frank Zappa poster haloing Katy's nearly unclad body. Katy still had some baby-fat on her and dressed only in a French maid's apron and her clogs she was full-breasted, desirable, and plush like a stuffed bear, a roly-poly sex toy. She was blushing and she didn't know what to do with her hands. She propped one on a hip in an approximation of coquettishness.

"This is all I had on under my coat," she tittered, but Jolly's degage reaction made her trail off, ambivalently.

"We have work to do," he said.

"Can't we fool around first? I'm safe right now," she said, disappointment growing in her like a cloud.

"After the experiment, maybe. It won't work otherwise."

"Jesus, it's not gonna work anyway," Katy said, throwing her coat back around herself.

"If you do not believe you better go," Jolly said as if he were a high priest.

"Ok, ok. Lemme stay, Jolly. I'll be good," she said, cinching the belt on her coat. "Whaddya want me to do?"

With the lights lowered and the candles lit and Jolly wearing only a light robe it really did seem like some kind of sacral rite, a black mass like in the Fantastic Features movies Katy had seen on TV. She was becoming interested. And, besides, Jolly's body, orphic itself, slim and muscular like she'd never seen it, was calling to her through that silky robe.

Jolly began to chant in some foreign tongue and Katy was duly impressed. This was not the awkward guy she'd been palling around with the past couple of years. Here was a new side--venerable, dark, dangerous--to him and it was attractive as hell.

The glass ball sat on a small tripod, seemingly made just for it. It still looked like some tony piece of room decor to her, but in Jolly's atmosphere of mystification she could imagine seeing it glow. She shook her head. Something was making her drowsy, her thoughts scrambled, her mind unclear.

The ceremony went on and on. Jolly earnestly chanted and exhorted and huffed and puffed until Katy thought she would die of fatigue, desire, boredom. It seemed, though, as if Jolly were growing frustrated, his cantellation broken and scattered. Nothing was happening, save for the languor, the muscle-cramping agony of sitting cross-legged for what seemed hours. The ball stubbornly refused to yield its secrets. It stayed dim, murky.

Finally, Jolly opened his eyes wide and shook his head. He leaned back on his hands and looked into Katy's face for a long moment.

"Something's not right," he said, almost tearfully.

"I'm sorry," Katy whispered.

"I'll have to work harder."

"You wanna, you know, fuck now?"

"Katy," Jolly said.

"*Don't mind me*," said a voice from the corner.

The two teens scrambled to their feet. In the murk, in the indistinct, clothes-strewn chair in the corner, sat a figure, darksome and obscure. Katy clutched Jolly's arm and pulled herself against him tightly. Some time passed. The murk did not lift. Their vision did not become clearer. The room smelled faintly of sweat and something else, something new, a metallic, chemically fusc.

Jolly swallowed. Then he squared his shoulders.

"Are you whom we have summoned?" Jolly asked, importantly.

"Who else?" the figure said.

"Jesus," Katy said.

"Hardly," the man said, standing.

He was dressed in too many clothes, layers of indefinite cloth, as if he had been swaddled. And he was portly, his belly swelling in front of him like a sandwich board. He held it proudly and his expression was one of diffidence and ennui. His face was wreathed in unkempt hair and he looked a little like a demented Sebastian Cabot, or maybe Santa Claus.

"What are you called?" Jolly asked.

"I am Angus," he pronounced.

"Angus. I've not heard of you."

The visitor waved a scunnery hand.

"I am one of the lesser arelim. You've probably heard of my big brothers, Harut and Marut. I just never got the press."

In truth Jolly had not heard of his brothers either, but he nodded appreciatively.

"You got anything to eat?" Angus said and stalked past them and down the stairs. They could hear him rummaging around in the icebox.

Jolly and Katy relaxed their grip on each other slowly. Katy gave her beau a sort of "now what?" look.

When they joined their guest downstairs he was seated at the kitchen table eating some leftover macaroni salad and he had a copy of Mr. Newbacon's *Sports Illustrated* spread out next to him.

"So," he expatiated around half-masticated food. "Whadja want?"

"Want?" Jolly said, thrown out of his holy reverie by his angel's apparent coarseness.

"Whadja call me for?"

Jolly had not thought that far ahead. He had spent so much time preparing for the summoning he had never speculated on what would happen if it worked.

"I, I really don't know," he sputtered.

"Good," Angus said. "Cuz I really don't like to do much." And here he punctuated his statement by raising up on one cheek and breaking wind loudly.

"Oh, good job, Jolly boy. You conjured a bum," Katy said.

"You two kids go on about your business," Angus said, his head bowed over the magazine.

"C'mon," Katy said, pulling Jolly's sleeve and leading him back to the bedroom.

They sat down on the bed and Jolly seemed a million miles away.

"Now what?" Katy said, explicitly.

"I don't know."

"Do you think we can send him back?"

"I don't know," he said again. He fell back onto the bed and stared at the ceiling as if the answer were there.

"Let's give him a task," Katy said after a few minutes.

"Like what?" Jolly answered with no interest.

"How about turning Melanie Traynor into a lizard?"

"Katy, I brought him here for a high purpose. I just don't know, right now, what that is."

"I don't think this angel is a high-purpose kind of guy."

Jolly sighed. He was deeply perplexed, disappointed, tired. It brought out Katy's nurturing instincts and re-engaged her libidinous nature. She began rubbing Jolly's stomach through his thin robe.

Getting no response she stood and again dropped her coat. Jolly stared at her, as if it were she he had just crystal-balled.

"Monsieur," Katy purred with a grin. "You perhaps need me to make up ze bed. Or do ze laundry? I could perhaps take that robe for you."

Despite his head being in the clouds his body remained earthbound, as evidenced by the rising formation under his robe. Katy pulled the robe open and stretched her near-naked plenitude over Jolly's muscular midsection. Her ample breasts spread across Jolly's stomach like a lambent salve. She writhed there.

When Katy started to fellate the prone archimage he began to come back to life. Soon he was an active participant, the physical contact the perfect anodyne to his mental unrest. He pulled Katy's plump round buttocks tightly forward. He sank his tongue into her mouth. He was almost angry, hungry for humanness.

When she mounted him and sat above him bucking like a being from elsewhere he knew an earthly pleasure which begged no spiritual intervention. He threw his loins upward with animalistic abandon.

They both became aware of the angel in the doorway at about the same time. Katy screamed and fell off the bed onto the floor. She gathered some clothing off the floor and held it against herself.

"Aww, don't stop, children," Angus said, biting into a tomato he held in one hairy paw.

"You bastard," Katy spat.

"Katy, some respect," Jolly said in his fluster.

"He's a goddam peeper," she countered.

"Well, it's certain you didn't call me to help you with your sex life," Angus said. "Most high school boys, that's what they want."

"Can you do that?" Jolly asked.

"Naw."

"What can you do? Give me some help here," Jolly said, forgetting the embarrassment of only a moment ago.

"Not much, I guess. I used to be pretty good at small things. Yardwork, repairs. I could probably lube your car, still."

"Great," Katy said. "An angelic grease monkey."

When Jolly's parents came home Angus moved into the bottom of Jolly's closet. It was a walk-in and he made a cubby-hole underneath the coats for himself. There he dragged in foodstuffs and magazines and soon the closet began to resemble the cave of some omnivorous and slovenly creature. Each day, after everyone went to work, Angus would sneak downstairs and spend the day eating and watching cable. Evenings he assisted Jolly with his homework, but, to be honest, he wasn't that bright and he was little help. Also, Angus had started to smell, something about him not quite clean. It was a fusty odor, a cross between cheese and floor wax.

Things went this way for a week or so.

One afternoon Jolly was reading one of his occult texts (he was looking for a remand spell) and Angus was sprawled on the bed looking at a *Playboy* magazine.

"Do you think she needs theanthropic aid?" he asked, holding up a glossy spread of a brunette goddess with one dainty hand curled into her own pubic forest.

"Angus," Jolly said with weary inspiration. "You need to do something. You can't just live here and sponge off us. Mom's getting suspicious about the amount of food missing."

"Your every wish is my command," he said, with mean-spirited irony.

"I mean it, dammit," Jolly said.

"Don't swear at an angel, you little jerk," Angus spat back. "I've been dead longer than you've been alive."

"Sorry, but you gotta earn your keep."

"Yeah, yeah. You don't even know what you want."

"Here," Jolly said suddenly and he rifled through his backpack until he found what he wanted. It was a mimeographed announcement about the play-writing contest. "Write a play for me." He thrust the paper under the angel's bulbous nose.

Angus read the rules over seriously. He grinned.

"I think I can do this," he said.

In later years Edward Newbacon told anyone who would listen that he divided his life into two parts. Before the play and after the play. This was an exaggeration for dramatic effect but it held a grain of truth. The play was a watershed event in his life, only because it marked the end of his angelic visitation, and perhaps the end of his days as a wide-eyed votary. But this is getting ahead of ourselves.

He had told Angus, and he didn't know where he got the idea, that he wanted a play about Beale Street.

"What's a white boy in the suburbs know about Beale Street?" Angus rightly asked him.

"Nothing," Jolly admitted. "I know it's part of black history, maybe this drowsy city's only interesting piece of the past. They had conjuremen back then, I think. And the blues, you know, that gave birth to rock and roll. And, besides, everyone else will be writing about yellow fever, or the Civil War, or Boss Crump." Jolly was only dimly aware of what these topics meant, also. "I'll distinguish myself by my disparity."

"You're just another white boy wanting to beggar his cool from black culture."

"Don't gimme a hard time about this, Angus."

"Awright," Angus said, reassuringly. "Beale Street it is."

Mrs. Parrish summoned Jolly to her desk after class one day. "Have you worked on your entry to the contest, Mr. Newbacon?"

"Yes, ma'am," he answered.

"Splendid," she bubbled. Honestly she hadn't counted on this at all.

"And what is your subject?"

"Beale Street."

Mrs. Parrish did not let a trace of disillusionment cross her bright smiling face. She did not betray for one moment the confidence she had placed in her pupil. Mrs. Parrish smiled and smiled and smiled.

Jolly nodded and left.

Katy had become more openly amorous and spent most her evenings either at the Newbacon's house or on the phone with Jolly. Signing off she would say, "Love ya," and once, he said the same back. Their sex life was put on hold, the angel proving to be an anerotic presence in their lives.

"You ever think about marriage?" Katy asked one night in the car on the way to Burger King.

"No," Jolly said.

"Don't freak. I was just cogitating out loud," she said.

One day Mrs. Parrish again called to Jolly as he was leaving.

"Tomorrow's the deadline, you know," she said.

"I know," Jolly said, but he had had no idea. It was not incumbent on him to pressure his angel.

So after school he found Angus in front of the TV answering every Jeopardy question with callous aplomb.

"What's new, Master?" the slatternly seraphim burped from his perch.

"Not much," Jolly said. "Clean up those potato chip crumbs before Mom comes home, how about it?"

"Yeah, yeah."

"Oh, and the play is due tomorrow. I hope you've been working on it."

"Done, done and done."

"Oh, good. Can I see it now?"

"I was fully aware of the deadline," Angus said, not even turning his head to speak. "I mailed in your entry this morning."

Jolly let a beat go by. He was appalled, slightly panicked.

"Mailed it where?"

"To Mrs. Parrish's home, of course," came the answer. "What is Paraguay?"

"What?"

"What is Paraguay?" the TV intoned.

Jolly stomped off to his room. He threw himself onto his bed and again sought the solace of the middle distance. His only hope was that his abhorrent angel was, against all probability, a writer of some aptitude. At least, he hoped, not to be embarrassed.

To be fair, the play probably is an underappreciated gem, maybe ahead of its time. It will never be judged by the world, however, never see itself trod across the boards of even a high school auditorium.

It is famous only for being abruptly obliterated.

It upset Mrs. Parrish, horrified the committee. And it destroyed Jolly.

It lives on only in whispered tales, tales told out of school, so to speak. Its vermiculate take on the English language, if not a new pidgin, if not *Angelspeak*, will never be debated. (Angus said that he wrote it first in Enochian and then translated it into English as best he could, using a Roget's and Jolly's high school dictionary.) Its immortality, its afterlife is only a whisper, a memory, as ethereal as dust, pixie dust. Angel dust.

REAL BEALE: A Tragicomedy

Newintown, the stranger approaches the modernartistic tourist center kiosk with minor trampidation.

The empirer looks upward only as faras the newman's goggles.

And l'etranger speaks first.

--This hear Beale Street?

--Beatles streak, yes.

--Much music, muchmuch, yes?

--There is music. Beatlesqueak.

--I have come far from afar, many miles.

--I coordinate with you. Well come.

--Thenkyu. I want to see.

--There is much to see depending, of course, on whooz doing the looking. See now repent later.

--I work only on the repent later plan. Where to begin? There is Bingo.

--Aye, forty-seven.

--Is club, is faymus.

--I know.

--You have tours...

--Tourettes, fuck cock balls, oh yes. Tourettes, little tours, get it?

--...busses...

--We've only just met, and yet...

--Where to begin? You are a god?

--The god's in the godhouse, counting up his money. You want, I'm summerizing, the whole encino, the trip to life fantastic. You want me to open up the gate for you, show you the Secret Beale, the one we keep under where?--under raps, under discos, under ground down. You want Cindy's sister, you want blow job. The Beale of His and Her Story. The horse and man, thee lushcribs, thee lux. This is what you are in your forner way, axing of me?

--Thenkyu, yes.

--Southern hospitalality. Pleezed, I'm sure.

--We see now.

--Wheezy now?

--Whee c.

--Aye.

--I.

--Under the B, Beale Street. You want maybe to see the Oscar, Madison Avenue Porn Emporium--it wasn't porn yesterday, the Rust Stadium where Red Rolly hit the ball seen round the corner, Smalley's maybe, Ssshwab's, Rev. Ike's mike, the Pope's nose, the monkey man's monkey, the soultakers the souldrivers, the sotweed shop, the donot stop, the place where the girls keep the heat, the well where da music cum from.

--For a start.

--Beale Street, Beale Street, give me your muddled mastiffs, your weak and lazy minds, two beers and a broom. I'm standing on your shoes, a pilgrimator, a man with a fancy, a fancy man.

--How bout something to eat?

--Whatcha got?

--Foodstuffs, manna live, dyspepsy, dyin' man's dinna, cheapjacks, crow, coke, coxcrow—

--Whatcha got?

--I got life brother, I got million dollar charm cuzzin.

--You know Callie Pidgeon?

--I know Ty Chee. One from column B. B for Beale Street.

--You wanna see Nekkid Ladies?

--Is it real?

--It's a chain, it's franchised, it's torn up torn down, reassembled as gentrified as the Gentries, reborn and rerealized. It's all that's left of dreams, son--Dream Lite.

--For this you wait on line.

--For everything you wait online. You weren't bored yesterday.

--Which board?

--The Board of Reconstitution for the Preservating Reservation of Real Beale. Purist colony for the sick of soul, son.

--Zounds right.

--You wanna see stars?

--C stars.

--We got stars, a star called Roofus, a star called Kansas. A star the size of a werewolf's penis. Hook up the wagons, Pa. We got stars for everybody. Can do a starry, starpitch, end up at The Start. Star the glaze? You wan' ice?

--I's. Eyes., Not everybody gonna wanna come.

--Thas true. Right as reign. You wanna start at BB's?

--Find.

--It's booked. Bookered.

There is a period of profound science between the toomen. Off in the distaff a sound of blooz music played backwards, satanism rolling in on twisted fermatas. The men listen and then don't.

The pro-privateer speaks.

--Ok, we can get you on the first bust outa here. All expenses paved by the Town Cuntzel. Whatsay?

--Have I seen Beale Street? Have I seen the real thing? Have I had an eggsperience, validated like a parking sticket?

--Have you dreamed? Have you hell-loose-inated? You trippin son? Beale Streetsa state of mine.

--You must be Tennessee.

--Why I wear the tuxedo, conjunction-junction. I'm the man, the first cousin of Two-Tone Tailor, mayor to the blues. I'm the son of the man wrote "She Caught the Kitty," Klaus Abovo's rite-hand band, the tale of the gator. The hobjobber, the Headcheese, the Head Beatler. I'm the One, son, and there ain't no Too.

--I've come too far.

--You past it.

--The past isn't passed, it isn't even frozen.

--Not leastways in the South.

--Not here.

--I believe my time is up, strainjer. Love to you. Stay offa Lonely Street.

--My sister come lookin for me, you say my name is Legend. I'm gone like the Dead.

--You sister?

--Nameza Ora.

--Naw.

--Sure as fire, friend.

--She fine, here tell.

--She tol me, come to town, look up Beale. The ghost'll welcome you.

--Whyncha say so firstly, brother?

--Make a difference?

--We got a back door, time machine. Krono discombobulator.

--Cost me?

--Got a soul?

--Lost it in a poker game with Old Hob hisself. Must be fitty years hence.

--Aw, hellzapoppin. C'mon.

And here the two join at the crooks and sautee crabfashioned through the Door into Summer, never to be seen again in this fair storyville and never thought of nomore.

Curtains.

Now it's up to you. Some said Jolly was channeling some demon spirit (this was in the heyday of the hysteria about the devil cults and such) and some said he didn't write it but found it in one of his esoteric texts. Angus insisted it sounded better in Enochian.

At any rate he was expelled from school, banished from the garden of public education. He got a job working at an Exxon station, pumping gas. He and Katy got married before she ever graduated and they had a boychild, Amos, within the year.

With no money and a valetudinarian youngster (Amos was pale and withered as if he hadn't stayed long enough on the vine and was constantly at the doctor's office) they were pretty miserable, but they still talked about the time they conjured an angel together and how that made them closer, closed them, made them what they are, whatever that may be. They are trapped in their own history, doomed, like the mariner primeval, to the telling, the fractured reiteration of their own parable.

"Tell me again about that last conversation you had with the angel," Katy will say some evening when Amos has finally settled down for a couple of hours of hiatal snooze.

"I caught him in my parents' room," Jolly always begins. "He was looking through my mother's underwear drawer, looking for dirty pictures, I'm betting. And I burst in on him, crazy with anger.

'You bastard-angel, you beat-up beatific,' I yelled. 'You old soak. You've ruined my life. They just kicked me out of school.'

'Cor!,' he responded. 'Sorry, Jake.'

'You're out. Now. Unfurl your filthy wings and fly outa here.' I bellowed.

'Hold on, chum.'

'I want you gone. Did you hear what I said? My life is ruined because of you and your dirty-minded play.'

'What's one life?' he said. 'What's one play?'

And I lunged for him--I meant to tear his impudent throat out--and he wasn't there. Just that easily he wasn't there. Gone in a puff of baby powder. Back he'd gone to Elysium or whatever halfway house they have for disembodied nitwits. And all that lingered was a faint aroma of overripe cheese."

"I love the way you tell that," Katy says, feeling amorous again, indefatigable she was in her physical needs.

She coils up next to him like a cat in heat, reaching for his manhood, the center of him, his root.

"I am a man," Jolly Newbacon says, lying back. "Just so."

"What's one play?" Katy Newbacon whispers, huskily, dreamily. "In the larger picture. What's one life?"

Scuff Maladicta:
A Ghost Story

--Beale Street a street of ghosts.

--Thas what I'm sayin.

--So.

--Just so.

--You gonna tell me bout it?

--Sure sure.

--You gonna tell me whas differen bout this ghost?

--Thas what I'm tellin you.

--Right.

--Was Squiggly Pete firs tol me.

--So you said.

--Lemme get on.

--Right.

--Was Squiggly Pete firs tol me. Says, Rolly tol him an Styx tol him, an back an back. So the story not so fresh anymo, I'm sayin.

--Uh huh.

--But there was a cat back then, musician, of course. Big man with the winds, I'm hearin, blow em like kingdom comin, any of em, big or small. Blow a barrel full.

     Got him a gig at one of the clubs, easy back then, lotsa clubs. Was sittin in with some of the best, yes, played with Lady Day I'm hearin, once anyway. On Beale tho he soloin lots, got himsef a rep, started regular work, name on the markee, that sort of thing.

     Course the ladies comin roun, back then, heh, they all over the musicians, musician bein bout the highest a black man get to, leastways on Beale, not sayin anything against your gangster, your club owner, your ball player. Musician bout the best, you know.

--Sure.

--One particular gal, you mighta heard tell, name Callie Pidgeon, took a real professional shine to this cat.

--Naw.

--Whatchoo mean, naw?

--Callie Pidgeon.

--Yeah.

--She Ricky Romito's gal.

--This before that.

--Ah.

--Anyway. Callie and this cat, Andrew Maladicta by name, called him Andy or Scuff, cuz he always scuffin his shoe to the beat, got one leg goin nineteen to the dozen, like he couldna sit still, like he got the devil in him, some say, took up with each other and it was fine, fine. Scuff and Callie, like it was meant to be.

Then Scuff's rep got bigger than Scuff, so to speak. Took him a high payin job at the best club on the Street, at Daddy's, his name on the sign as big as Daddy's hisself. He was king of the Street, see, and Callie, she relegated to minor status, sorta, a jewel on his finger, somethin on his arm for the end of the night, when the music was over. And Callie she a patient woman, she adored her man and didn't rightly care too much about the talk, the talk what said she was jes a toy for the king and not his only toy.

Well, things proceeded all right for a while, status quo maintained and all, and one afternoon Callie come home early and there was Scuff in the all and all doin one of the barmaids from the club, he blowin on his tenor sax and she on somethin else altogether, making music twice at once, see what I mean.

Callie she jes walked out. Thas all she did, she that strong. Didn't look back, didn't need to. She cry all right. She cry two, three days straight. But it was over and, far as she concerned, that club, that hornblower now off limits.

She moved on, our Callie did.

Then somethin happened.

--You gonna tell me?

--Yeah, yeah. Jes makin sure you still listenin.

--I'm here.

--Somethin happened. Somethin dreadful.

They found that hornblower, that Andrew Maladicta, with his head stoved in. Found him in that high falutin apartment with his head stoved in, beat to death he was with one of his own horns, a sousaphone I think they said it was.

--A whatsit?

--Sousaphone, I think they said.

--Don know it.

--Me neither. Big horn, I'm thinkin, cuz his head was right stoved in.

--Couldna been no accident.

--Naw.

--Huh.

--Dead he was, murdered in blood colder than the world's heart. Some of his things missin, sure, some rings and what, but ruled it a passion crime they did. Fingered Callie quicker than snatch, took her down to the jail and put her there and forgot her like she was a song from befo the blues.

And there she woulda stayed but for some right-thinkin detective who put the T-O-D at bout the exact time Callie was workin her twelve hour shift at the restaurant. Did I say Callie was a waitress?

--Naw. You sure this is Callie Pidgeon? She weren't no waitress, she a stripper.

--This before that.

--Awright.

--She was a waitress at the BrownTown Downtown, Matt Smiley's place.

--I hearda it.

--She was there anyway, couldn't a murdered that sax player, you see. And, bless them, they let her go. Tol her to watch herself anyway for good measure, but set her free as the breeze. She almos celebrated, cept she still blue over Scuff an all, she did love the cheat.

Went back home, brooded a few mo days and then, was back at Matt's like nothin ever happened. She a tough one, Callie was.

Coupla weeks later, it was, Callie was closin up the restaurant one night, sent the dishwasher on home and stayed by herself to lock up, doin the last minute addin up of the cashbox, and the restaurant quiet as a tomb. She sittin there at a table, hummin "Mississippi Lowdown Blues" to herself, scratchin on the pad with a pencil stub, when she hear a whisperin somewhere behind her. Sound like the wind through a tin can, somethin like. Sound like someone sayin her name, a high thin sound.

She look around, no one there, course. She go back to figgerin.

Again, a whisperin. And, this time, the tinkle of metal pots, like a windchime music.

This time Callie stood up, peered back through the openin there into the kitchen. The swingin door movin maybe ever so slightly.

Callie not the spook-easy type, she felt still the little hairs on her neck a-dancin. She put her hand there like you do at the end of a hard day an she stood there thinkin to herself. You ol fool, Callie said, sorta half to comfort herself and half to think somethin other than spectre speculation.

An shortly after she locked up and went on home.

It was there, in Callie's apartment over the pawn shop, when she had slipped down to her finer things, she heard the whisper again, this time closer by, and somethin like a cat's whisker against her forearm.

She jerked back, spoke out. --Who there?

She standin by her bed, nothin on her but those teddy things, light as spider web, an she there in the moonlight, can you picture it?

--Yeah.

--An she hear the voice, the whisper sayin clear as night, Mm, mm, you shor look good.

Well, she shrank back from the bed from where that voice emanatin and she could make out there in the dim a shape under the quilt there in her bed, the shape of a man. And then, like her eyes were just adjustin to the dark or more like he just appearin out of the ether, there was that polecat, Andrew in her bed. His ghost mindja.

--Man.

--Yeah. And he was naked, there, this undead thing, and seem like he tryin to coax her into the bed, like the line between this world and the next not pronounced enough to hinder a man when he longin for some of the good stuff, like this saxman so horny Lucifer hisself coulna hold him.

--Wha she do?

--She backed off slowly I tell you.

--Sure.

--Keepin her eye on that lascivious devil. She backed all the way across the room till her rear hit the divan and she sat down slowly like she need to keep him in her sight.

Took her a few minutes, understandably, fore she could speak, but when she could she did.

She said, You come back jes to get back in the sack with me, Andy?

He say, Good enough reason, sugarpie.

She say, Naw, man, you ain't conquered death for a slap an tickle.

He think a minute and say, You right. I come back for larger business. I needs to catch me a murderer.

Who done it, Andy, she say, and checked herself, cuz she could already hear her sweetenin up to him again.

Caynt tell you yet, sweetheart. Gonna catch him, make him fess up.

Why can't ya tell me, she say.

Don want him warned, sugarpie. Don wan no one knowin yet.

Needless to say she say she won tell and he say he playin it safe and after further ranglin, him trying still to get her to climb into her warm bedclothes with him, uncovering his ghostly mantool, showin her the ol tricks still apply, that sorta thing, all in vain, she strong as I said befo, he drifted out into the night, like a sulfrous wispa smoke.

Callie she stay up all night that night so when she gots to work the next night she was draggled and spent and she had missed all the commotion and she was muzzy headed and needed to be sat down and tol twice everything but the jist of if was that Matt Smiley had absquatulated outa there. He gone on the evenin stage. He didden even leave a bad smell.

--Matt Smiley.

--The one.

--Disappeared?

--Yeah.

--Wait. I heared that, nows you say it. Some mystery where he went. Left his store and things behind and never heared from again.

--Right.

--You tellin me that mixed up with this parable?

--Thas right.

--You gonna tell me he killed Andrew Malacat?

--Maladicta. Lissen.

--Huh.

--Matt Smiley was gone allright. Gone like the sunset and it was years befo anyone put 2 and 2 together and pieced together what transpired.

Sometime in the early hours of that mornin, the story goes, Matt Smiley was in the Browntown, jes him and a busboy name of Jonny Dingo, makin up the soupa the day or somesuch, when they heared the bell tinkle on the front door like someone come in, though they both knew they locked that door. Matt looked at Jonny and Jonny looked at Matt and both managed weak smiles.

They checked out front and there wasn't nobody there that they could see.

--That they could see, heh.

--You got it.

They turned and toddled back through the swingin doors into the kitchen to re-commence their ministrations on that soupa the day or somesuch and he was there.

--The ghost. The dead man.

--Yessir.

He was a-standin next to a big table they used to roll out their dough and cut things up and stuff and he was holdin a big kitchen knife like they used to debone hams and such and he was smilin a smile straight from the firey place and both employer and employee like to do number two right there.

Matt Smiley spoke first cuz he was used to givin the orders not takin em. He say, Maladicta.

And Maladicta say back, Here, in the deterioratin flesh.

Cuz now that he say that they see that sure nough he one rottin specimen, patches round his cheeks, on his forearms, betwixt his fingers, fairly hangin there like raw chicken.

(Not what Callie saw, see, cuz he was shape-shiftin, using what needs be when needs be.)

An his toothy grin was rotten too, grey like tombstones, and the stink comin off him was like grim death itself, cuz it was.

And Matt Smiley say again, Maladicta. You come back fo me? You my psychopomp?

You betcha, the dead sax player say.

--You betcha?

--Yeah.

--All right.

--You betcha.

Whatchoo gonna do? Matt Smiley rightly wanted to know.

Gonna skin you like a lamb, Matt Smiley say, or leastwise, what Jonny say he say.

--Ize gonna ask you that? All this come from that busboy?

--Yeah.

--What happened to him?

--He hospitalized for long time. They put his ass on the thirteenth floor till he stop talkin constant fool talk--they say he talked for eight straight years, Bible talk, hellfire, Jabberwock, till one day he just stopped, looked around and they call for the doctor and he say you in charge? to the doctor and the doctor allowed as to how he was and Jonny stood straight up and said I got a story to tell.

--Huh. So this all come from him.

--This part, yeah.

--Huh.

--So where was I?

--Skin you like a lamb.

--Right.

An Matt Smiley picked up a cleaver nearby and said, Devil take me.

An Maladicta say, Yessir he will.

An Matt lunged at the phantom an course his thrust with that bloody cleaver passed through the airy body of the dead musicman and Matt did now tremble with the fear of death.

An now, so Jonny tells it, the ghostly Mr. Maladicta swelled up like a parade balloon, grew twice his normal height and stood over that cowerin restauranteur with his bonin knife raised high. His putrescent flesh bout drippin off his bones, his mouth a maw of hellishness, teeth like a torture rack dribblin spittle. He rose up above him like a shade's shadow, obliteratin all around, he say.

--What?

--Thas all we know.

--Whatchoo mean, thas all we know?

--Busboy passed out. Woke up his boss was gone. Absquatulated. Started right in to ravin, off his head jes like that.

--Smile run away? Or dead? Eaten by that ghoul?

--Don know.

--Aw, man. They never found him, no?

--Naw. Never a trace, not a hair.

--Why he do it?

--Not for certain, suspect he in love with Callie, suspect he defendin her honor, in his way.

--An his way entail stovin in heads.

--I imagine.

--Man.

--And Callie?

--You know that. Became a stripper, mobster's moll, disappeared hersef some years later.

--Huh.

--Thas right.

--The ghost of Beale Street.

--One of.

--One of.

--Thas right.

Seth Adamson's Blues:
A Diablerie

The country they came from had lost its pride. Its language, its culture, its people had become the butts of jokes, an international cause for jest. This lack of respect had translated into a feeling of ridiculousness at home, a feeling of inappropriateness and marginalization and inanity, and this led to many defections, much expatriation.

No, the twentieth century had not been kind to this little kingdom. If thought of at all it was for the many jokes done in its name. Almost no one knew its breathtaking geography, its place in the European market. No credit was given for its marvelous sausages, its influential opera, its world-class athletes (not least of which was Ednay and Berthild Glek, the number-one-ranked synchronized swimming team).

Ask any seventh grader where it was and the answers would be wide-ranging in their incorrectness, their absurdity.

So it was that Seth Adamson and his wife Lilith (their adopted Anglicized names) came to America in the 1970s. So it was that they landed, with all their possessions in two cardboard suitcases, in a flophouse in the southwest quadrant of Memphis, Tennessee.

They spoke very little English, they spoke an English which sounded like the muddled coo of pigeons. They tried to get by with their native tongue, but few people spoke it at all and fewer still spoke it without tittering. Few people in Memphis, Tennessee, at this time in history, spoke their language. It was almost a dead tongue. Seth and Lilith, while very happy to be in America, the home of Elvis Presley and John Travolta, the home of *The Beverly Hillbillies* and John Wayne, had a tough row to hoe.

The near-derelict hotel where they stowed their gear and slept (at least that first night) the sleep of the near-dead was called the Akimbo Arms, though Godknowswhy. Its proprietor, a Mr. Grimus, was a bent-backed, wizened puppethead, with a fondness for ethnic jokes and canned meats. He never failed to spout a witticism about Seth and Lilith's homeland when they passed through his polluted lobby, grinning with mossy teeth and approximating an expansiveness which only accentuated the yawning lacuna of cultural differences between him and them and in microcosm illuminated their dilemma.

The dilemma was slow to dawn on the couple not due to any dimness on their part but because they kept an almost Oriental cheery outlook on most of life, also a product of the society they hailed from. They were cheery to a fault.

It was their intention to begin their lives anew in Memphis, Tennessee. It was their intention to make a name for themselves in the business which to their innocent minds was exemplified by Memphis, Tennessee, a business which propagated Memphis' finest export, the rock progenitor himself, Elvis Presley. They were naive for two reasons and here they are: Their musical heritage was aborn from their dying culture, a music, when not opera, as tiresome, as repetitive, as lachrymose, as cacaphonic as the worst of polka or rap, a music not too far advanced from the banging together of two rocks accompanied by the howling of wild animal disembowelment. And secondly, maybe most importantly, at this point in history, at this slippery point, Memphis, Tennessee was about as musical-savvy, as musical-appreciative as the continent of Atlantis.

Elvis was dead. Beale Street was dead. The blues were singing the blues. Where was the musical future? Certainly not in the stiff, uncertain hands of Seth and Lilith Adamson. It lay elsewhere or it did not lay at all.

At any rate, now:

Seth and Lilith set their suitcases on the dusty counterpane of their puny bed and smiled at each other with weary fondness. They fell into each other's arms at The Arms as the saying goes and it goes because it is appropriate and gay and they made love in dusty abandonment before falling into aforementioned slumber. In the morning of the second day they awakened early but not before old Sol who strained to furnish a ray of light through the near-obscured windowpane though a small ray was all the couple needed to feel hopeful and full of gusto and ready to face their first full day in their new home.

Seth looked at Lilith and Lilith at Seth and the spark between them was all about aspiration and faith and Memphis was not without either even for its own denizens but it took the heart of a child and the head of a bull to hold out if one (or two) was from where the couple was from and fixing to try their hands at a business which had defeated so many others, broken dreams and splintered spirits. But, if music was not to be their ticket to the promised land, could they get there all the same? Keep in mind Columbus' misdirected good fortune, the whole country then the product of a miscue which turned out all right depending on which side of the ethnocentric fence you are a-sitting on.

Let them go on.

Beale Street, Street of Myth and Home of the Blues, was a block and a whistle from The Akimbo Arms and it was there that Seth and Lilith headed on that first morning-- after breakfasting at a diner where they made *faux pas* after *faux pas* concerning what was on the menu and what was in their hungry heads, ordering first one native dish and then another (smoked squirrel sausage, buttered cornhusk, jellied liver) before settling on ham and eggs and grits which they found delectable. The instruments they carried would not be familiar on Beale but this would not be their defeat, no. Seth played the harmonitar (it looked like a potato with a snout) and Lilith the squeege, small wind instruments both, like recorders but uglier, and sounding like miniature bagpipes played through a dustbuster. Together they made quite a shivaree.

They walked onto historic Beale that dimly lit morning like dustbowl Okies come to the big city. What they found were boarded-up storefronts, giant pits where buildings formerly stood, a sprinkling of winos, one lone nightclub (The Rat Seller) not opened yet, and a drygoods store which seemed to be a cornucopia of all manner of buyables. The smiles on their tight little faces froze into Dr. Sardonicus rictus, their cheeriness undampened but quizzed and found unprepared. They shuffled forward like the last people on the planet, looking from one painted-over window to another, Sweeney's snack bar boarded up now, the lights out at the Daisy, the dust settled in every empty honkytonk on Beale, the death now long-forgotten and seldom mourned. The end.

They sat on the curb and spoke not at all.

Finally, Seth said, with hearty aplomb,

"Well, we come back later to Atray's."

And, Lilith nodded and the smile stayed put.

Philbert "Cornbread" Slunt affected white suits and a cock-of-the-walk strut which went along with his reputation as a street hustler. A man given to the grift and the con, not too handy with either, a small operator with big-time dreams. Like the street itself Cornbread had seen better days.

Beale Street was Cornbread's street and it was his and that was the way it was. He never gave a thought to moving on, to finding a better place to work his game. They knew him there, he had carte blanch and he knew better than to put it before the horse or look the horse in the mouth. He was wise to the ways.

When he first laid eyes on Lilith Adamson he was a man smitten, a man gone past loony. He barely saw the sawedoff husband by her side, if he registered him at all he registered him as one might a shadow, something dark on the edge of vision. Instead his eyes traced the line of lithe grace which was the cutout image of the wife, the willowy sexiness of a woman who came a long way and came up empty. In her forced cheerfulness, in her unplumbed, inchoate resignation, Cornbread Slunt found a devil's playground, a woman wanting. Or so he imagined.

For days he watched them drag their strange instruments up and down Beale, turned back once and again at The Rat Seller, but every day back again with those near sickly smiles pasted on their pasty faces. For days Cornbread formulated a plan to invite himself into their lives, for he saw with a hustler's canny cunning, that if he was to get to the woman he would also have to get to the man. Through him to her.

Seth and Lilith sat on the stoop of an abandoned building and watched the starving pigeons pick at imaginary crumbs near the statue of W.C. Handy. They spoke little and nibbled at cheese sandwiches they had picked up at a soup kitchen at a downtown church. It was quiet on Beale Street. As quiet as a sleeping boa.

From westwards, from the end of the street, maybe from the roiling river itself, an energy seemed to gather and move their way. They squinted in its direction and held their forage frozen near their lips. Something like a tumbleweed, or a miniature tornado was developing on the fabled street and moving in a consistent fashion down the center of the pavement. Something so white as to be blinding, as to be the center of a profound blindness, a ball of light perhaps, a phosphorescent corporation.

As it neared it shapeshifted; it took on human form. It was a man, a peculiar man, a man come some distance to alleviate their woes, a savior no less, so they imagined. The day was as still as aforementioned and a white form moved their way and became a man right before them in their sight.

The now distinctive individual stopped and grinned a grin full of salvation and hospitality. Seth and Lilith Adamson bloomed in its lambent glow. They rose as if drawn by a tractor beam and the smiles among the trio of new-met faces were incandescent, a TVA of power and illumination.

"Cornbread Slunt," the fantasy formulated.

And the Adamsons thought they were victims once again of the language barrier, once more mystified by their ignorance. This was a curious expression indeed.

"My name is Cornbread Slunt," the vision now elucidated, still with the glowing blessing of his happy mask.

"Ah," Seth Adamson said, "Seth and Lilith."

Lilith, Cornbread Slunt, rolled around in his batty belfry. It sounded like the formulation of all nature, a sound as sweet as rainfall or puppies crying.

"Charmed," he said and kissed the small snappable fingers of Lilith's left hand.

Lilith felt a tingle in her brow and wondered at this strange Memphis man with the European manners and the crisp white suit.

"You are not from here I surmise," Cornbread went on.

"From far away, yes," Seth said.

"What brings you to Beale Street?"

Seth Adamson struggled with his American diction, desiring to impress, to not embarrass his bride and himself and by extension his lost homeland with his unawareness.

"We must leave home. Must make music in new land, right away. We play much music. Songs and, um, alladbays."

Cornbread thought for a moment.

"You must be very talented," he brought out.

The Adamsons smiled.

And Lilith spoke: "My bridegroom very good, oh yes."

Her voice, like dragging a light chair across a wood floor, gave Cornbread a tremble down deep. In the root of his manhood where he went not often.

"You are modest, lady. I would love to hear you play."

"Here?" Seth asked shyly, but with a new hopefulness.

"Everyone plays on the street here. This is Beale Street, home of music, the place where music was midwived. Please, unsheath your instruments and proceed."

The Adamsons unzipped their cases and pulled out their alien implements and Cornbread Slunt was wide-eyed with anticipation and puzzlement.

Of course, what the Adamsons brought forth was something quite different from music and Cornbread was digging deep into his actorly gifts to keep a pleasant visage as the sounds cascaded around him, a catfight echoing off the boarded-up storefronts, resounding down the bricked alleyways, bouncing off the trusting, generous facade of Mr. Handy. Mr. Handy did not blanch. It was a noise from Hell and the Adamsons produced it with such reckless abandon that Cornbread Slunt was momentarily sidetracked and flummoxed in his strategy. He was, in short, frightened. Were these demons afore him? He put his bony hand over his palpitating heart and breathed deep from his abdomen, regaining his poise.

At last they desisted. And stood there smiling with expectation.

Cornbread held himself inert for a moment. He then reached very deliberately into his jacket pocket and pulled out a silk handkerchief which he raised to the dry corner of his eye and there dabbed at an imaginary saline drop. He shook his great thespian's head. He took a deep breath.

"I am in awe," he said.

"You like?"

"I am, ah, in awe."

"Americans like?"

Cornbread paused the pause of a Gielgud pause.

"Something better," Cornbread assured them. "*Memphians* like."

"Ah," Seth Adamson sighed, as if this were in truth some deep promise.

Lilith stood there twinkling, looking from man's face to man's face.

And Cornbread cupped his hand around the rounded, smooth skin of her bicep and inwardly swooned, and then a second later he put the other hand on Seth's shoulder.

"I will find a place for you here. I will find you an audience."

Seth and Lilith could not sleep that night and sat on their unyielding bed gazing out the soiled windowpane at the big goose moon. Perhaps it was moonmagic which infected them now and hindered slumber or perhaps it was new promise, exhilaration, agitation. This new-found home was proving to be a not-so-hard nut to crack.

Seth reached over and took Lilith's delicate hand (the hand which manipulated the difficult keys of her beautiful squeege) in his. She leaned her tangled hair onto his shoulder.

"Ah, sweetcakes," Seth said. "This new friend is very good."

"Esyay, imple--"

Seth interrupted his enthusiastic wife.

"In American, dear one."

"Yes. He is very good, my Ethsay." And she exhibited a dreaminess of gaze hitherto unknown in her emotional repertoire, and if Seth were not caught up in his own stargazing he may have wondered at his wife's sigh and blush.

The dutiful husband reached over and undid the buttons of his wife's muslin shirtfront. Her tactful cupfuls of breast stood naked in the moonlight, their ageless and eternally perpendicular nipples casting charcoal shadows against her white skin.

Lilith scrutinized her husband's grey-flecked pate as he bent his head to her bosom. She put affectionate fingers in his hair and whispered to him.

"My husband, my life, ah, my sweet eggplant."

There was a coy knock on their door that next morning. When Seth opened it, having hurriedly thrown a spidery robe over his hirsute nakedness, there stood (if this does not imply an erect humanoid posture) the Heep-like figure of Mr. Grimus.

"Good morning, munchkins," he sparkled. "Up and at em?" he inquired looking Seth up and down and transferring his steady gaze in a decidedly lascivious manner to the sheeted, seated form of Lilith still in bed.

"Yes," Seth said, smiling.

"You have a guest in the lobby. I, of course, assured him he could not possibly want you as you were new to this country and knew no one. But he insists there is no mistake and wishes to see you, post haste."

"Thank you, thankyou very mush," Seth said backing away from the door as if Mr. Grimus would close it. He turned to his wife and clapped his hands in delight. Lilith in turn clapped hers and the sheet fell away and Mr. Grimus gasped an old man's gasp and Seth quickly, smilingly, scooted to the door and closed it in his landlord's old hounddog face.

Cornbread Slunt was like a single, scrubbed-clean spot on a dingy surface. His beaming white suit stood in stark contrast to the shabby lobby which was now a theatrical background and his smile, the smile of the wolf if the wolf had a goldcapped tooth, drew the Adamsons forward as if under a spell.

"Good morning, fine people," Cornbread began, taking Lilith by the forearm and steering her into a musty armchair. Seth stood by grinning.

"As you rested in the sweet arms of Morpheus the wheels of business have been indisputably turning. Your business, that is. I figure a quick breakfast at the Arcade, over which I shall spill forth the plans for your future."

The couple was led like puppies to the restaurant and into a booth, where they ordered their new standard fare, triple servings of sweet buttered grits.

"The long and short of it, my dulcet immigrants, is that I have secured for you an audition, as we call it here in the land of the free and musical, and if all goes well, as I assure you it will, you could be performing, on stage in front of an appreciative audience by nightfall." Cornbread sat back and smiled across the grit steam at the thunderstruck faces of our heroes.

"I--I--I am without speech," Seth blurted. "Mr. Cornbread, I, I am without speech."

"There now, Seth my boy, do not blow a gasket. It is your talent which will lead you to the promised land. I am but a conductor on the way, who may, I add humbly, grease the tracks."

Lilith squirmed in her seat like an adolescent in church. Cornbread sent a quick wink in her direction before downing the rest of his tepid joe.

The club where the couple was now led was not like a club at all. It was a partially dilapidated house on a city street amid other partially or fully dilapidated houses and the only feature to distinguish it from someone's sorry residence was a small placard next to the propped open front door, hand-painted in pale blue, bearing the single word, "Rix."

"I thought, was thinking, we would play The Rat Seller. I mean I thought we play Beale?" Seth spoke automatically without thought to the appreciation they felt for their new Memphis agent.

"You've heard of Off-Broadway, Seth?" Cornbread said. "This is Off-Beale, or Off-Off-Beale, if you prefer."

"It is wonderful," Lilith said, elbowing her hesitant husband, who had never heard of Off Broadway, but, if it were a club on Beale, he'd rather play there.

They stepped through the door into a dimly lit cave of a room, where they found a couple of aluminum tables, held together with duct tape, surrounded by mismatched kitchen chairs. What space there was between tables was dusty and littered with mouse droppings. Still, the focus of the room was a raised platform, shoved against one wall, about three feet by eight feet, on which sat a battered drumkit--one bass, one snare, a high-hat.

From a backroom came a presumably human groan followed by a shuffling sound as if someone were sweeping up. Emerging through a curtained doorway came the proprietor of Rix, a three hundred pound woman of indeterminate age, hairless as a Chihuahua and wearing enough makeup for three three-hundred pound women.

"Shit," she said, in greeting. "It's too goddam early." She stuck a puckered paw in their direction and when no one took the proffered handshake Cornbread bent to it and kissed its downy sausages.

"Lady Madeline, Seth and Lilith Adamson," Cornbread said as if introducing royalty.

"Pleezed," Lady Madeline said.

"Yes," Seth said, grinning. And recovering his manners he bent to repeat Cornbread's gracious gesture. As his mouth brushed the plump hand, Lady Madeline extended one finger and gently wiped it across his lips.

"Let's show what we came to show," Cornbread said, hustling the couple onto the stage and helping uncrate their instruments. When the foreign musical instruments were revealed Lady Madeline's eyes widened and she cocked a quick glance toward Cornbread.

He smiled confidently.

The couple, nervous at first, when instrumented, took on a professional countenance as Lady Madeline and Cornbread settled onto a couple of rickety chairs. Lady Madeline sat hers like a mattress balanced on a bottle of wine.

The whine which emerged from those strange windbags filled that tiny room the way a laboratory beaker is filled with acrid smoke. Lady Madeline's eyebrows bounced up and down, her nose scrunching as if she were about to sneeze, her blubbery lips flicking here and there, the overall effect appearing as if the poor woman was bilious.

Amid the cacophony a sort of music surfaced and Lilith took short breathers to spit out peculiar lyrics of her own devising, punctuating the din with a high-pitched, prissy voice.

Innerday at noon

Eeze me Squay, please

Honey I do lather me

In the ayday, yeah

In the ayday.

When it was over the Adamsons beamed at their new friends, proud of their handiwork, expectant, happy. They smiled like birds whose nest is heavened in the heart of purple hills.

Lady Madeline managed a burnished beam and slowly, like a storm brewing, lifted her bulk from its precarious perch. She grunted as she stepped onto the stage.

She walked over to Lilith and looked her deep in the face. She ran a glance over her entire body and then with two fat hands she tugged Lilith's peasant blouse off her shoulders until it uncovered a lovely little valley of cleavage.

Lady Madeline looked to Cornbread who smiled in return, their secret code lost on the bewildered musicians.

"Be rat back," Lady Madeline said and lumbered off the stage and through the curtain. Cornbread rose and followed as if signaled.

When the two were out of earshot, in the backroom of the "club" where there were stacks of old boxes and a hotplate and small refrigerator, the alopecic proprietress turned to Cornbread and smirked.

"You said you needed an act," Cornbread began. "Something new."

"This sure is new, man," Lady Madeline said shaking her great head. "What we gonna do with these oddballs, huh?"

Cornbread stood silently by, well versed in the lady's ways, knowing she was cooking up a scheme.

"I tell you what we gonna do," she said finally. "We gonna lose that pipsqueak husband. We gonna let the chicky bird sing. We gonna emphasize her luscious chests, and we gonna back her with Willy and Buck and let her sing some American words. Whatchoo say to that, Cornbread?"

Cornbread smiled an oleaginous smile.

"Sounds good to me, Mam."

"You know it does."

"Let me handle the husband. He'll understand; it's her big break."

Seth was as cheerless as Eeyore but he smiled tenderly at his wavering wife. She looked into his eyes with years of warmth.

"I do not do this without you," she said.

"This is big chance. We make it this way."

"Thas right, Seth," Cornbread put in. "We start this way. Get Lilith's career off the ground and bring you in later as the coo de grass. Once we got her established the world's our oyster. We'll be the talk of Beale. Hell, Beale, we'll take this act on the road. They'll be toasting us in the finest halls in America. Baton Rouge. Muscle Shoals. Jackson."

"You sure, husband mine?" Lilith asked, touching his cheek.

"We do this," he said, and he kissed her now uncreasing forehead.

That very night Lilith put on her best blouse and sweater (a native "skirlock" with crocheted scenes of battle) and dirndl and Seth followed her out into the twilight heading for her first professional appointment.

Cornbread took her arm and they walked on ahead. Seth hung back, following, not wanting to intrude on their transacting, as the Memphis agent whispered encouragement, advice and small woo into Lilith's undercroft ear.

Lilith glanced back over her shoulder numerous times and each time Seth sent her a smile, a strained moue of reassurance.

From half a block away Rix did not look too bad, a soft yellow bug light on its porch drawing folks in. There was almost a festiveness about it.

Inside they were greeted by Lady Madeline who now wore a wig of yellow hair-like twine piled high on her enormous head. It reminded Seth of the hayricks back home.

"Honey," she said, pulling Lilith ahead and into the back room, leaving Seth standing uncertainly in the doorway. Cornbread indicated with his eyes that Seth was to find himself a place in the audience.

In the backroom there was the sour smell of tamales cooking and a toothless old black woman looked up from her grill as the musician and her boss conferred quickly.

"We gotta get rid of this sweater first off."

Lilith smiled ambivalently as Lady Madeline tossed the garment onto some boxes. The large woman then unbuttoned the top two, then three buttons of Lilith's blouse and stood back a bit to survey.

"Well, it ain't exactly Las Vegas, but you look tasty enough. Uh, and Honey, we gonna try without the squeezebox tonight," she said taking the instrument and placing it on top of the sweater. "My boys'll back you. You just sing a bit--you know, make it up for now and we'll teach you some real stuff, some blues numbers later on."

Lilith felt panic well up in her like vomitus. Her eyes shot around. Where was Seth? She suddenly didn't understand anything. And then, just as suddenly, she was dragged onto the stage and Lady Madeline was talking, getting the crowd to simmer down, and she was standing in front of a hunchbacked drummer and a guitarist, who looked about thirteen, and they were ignoring her and looked about as uninterested in her as in the instruments in front of them. Their eyes were druggy brown, like the river to their right.

"All the way from the exotic East," Lady Madeline was saying to the semi-hushed room. "Flown in for your delectation, sparing no expense to bring you the newest talent. And without further ado, here she is, the Pride of Peking, the Yokohammer Warbler, Little Mama Adamson."

There was a smattering of half-hearted handclaps from the six or seven folks gathered there who still had heads above table level.

The room held its breath. There was a stillness all around and out of the void Lilith could hear Seth's steady breathing. From somewhere out in the fog he watched and waited.

Then there was a beat like the club had a heart and the unearthly roar of an electric guitar and Lilith was awash in sound, a swaying, bumpy sound which pulled at her clothes and thumped behind her ears. There was something persuasive about it, raw and ragged, rough and rumbly, insinuating itself into her blood.

She turned and looked at the drummer and where there was formerly a sleepy gnome there was a rhythm machine and the boy on the guitar was all dreamy concentration as his fingers slid fluently over the strings, drawing sounds from it which came from some dark place. The drummer looked at her expectantly and nodded his head repeatedly. It dawned on her she was supposed to sing.

Her mind was murk. Then, out of some Beale Street diablerie, the music worked inside her and she let out a slippery first phrase, more a purr than a word. And then, she was singing. Nonsense, at first, but vaguely tunefully, her cat-screech an offbeat complement to the percussive playing.

Weeee, yeah, oh long

Yeah, weeee, oh oh oh

I ahhh, oh I

Got em got em, weeee

And as the music got smokier, the room friendlier, Lilith found herself swaying and crooning. She could feel the sweat on her chin and chest and tiny rivulets ran down her blouse and she put a shy hand there and felt the moisture and it was good and she let her fingers linger there and the crowd moaned and something was happening.

She sang:

I need a man

I need a man

Every night in this
new land

I need a good man.

And the room was
hers and her squall found
its place and the audience
applauded more than
half-heartedly at the
end and when it was
all over Lilith stood
soaked in sweat
and adoration and
slowly she came
back to herself
and found herself
wet and half
exposed, her shirt
open, her dirndl
un-dirndled and
her pretty legs on
view. She gasped
and ran from the

stage, through the curtain, past the toothless cook and
out the back door into the Memphis night.

Every morning Lilith went to Rix to practice with
her new band, which was now called the Tomcats. And every
evening, except Mondays, she sang her heart out to growing
crowds on the modest stage at the club.

For the first week or so Seth accompanied his wife to
the practices, his enthusiasm diminishing incrementally. Soon
he stopped going to the practices, but went every night to the
actual performance where he sat developing his new fondness

for American beer which was given to him free as partial
compensation for his wife's act.

And every morning Cornbread arrived at the Akimbo
Arms precisely at nine to squire his protégé to their appointed
place. And, for a while, he spent some small time trying to
convince Seth to join them.

"Come, my man, we're cooking up some new numbers
I think you're gonna find delicious. And we've added a verse
to 'That Noodlehead Epaminondas Blues' which should be a
real crowd pleaser. Whaddya say?"

From out of the purple funk of his hangover Seth
burped and shook his head.

"You go now. Do good."

He watched as Cornbread put a steadying hand on his
wife's lower back and the two sashayed out.

Seth, when he was sobered up, spent much time
worrying about his wife's newfound sexiness. Her act was
getting more and more suggestive and her lyrics openly
sensual. Last night she drew her hand up her thigh and her
fingers were dangerously close to her treasure as she exposed
a tantalizing corner of blue striped panties. And this while
she sang about "touching me, touching me." Where was it
coming from? When asked she grew embarrassed and said she
had no idea she was acting in any way that was improper. It
was the music carrying her away, she said. And Seth was left
to wonder if she were pretending. Certainly their own sex life
had become a frozen, desiccated thing.

Actually it was a little of both. Lilith was carried
away by the devil's music--sometimes on stage she wanted to
fully expose herself, she wanted that kind of approval from
the audience. She could feel it in herself sometimes, welling
up like an orgasm, and indeed sometimes on stage she felt
close to coming, one tiny touch of her sweaty fingers would

accomplish it. And, mercy, she wanted that sometimes, to come on stage, in the heat, with all those eyes on her. She couldn't talk to Seth about it--it was so foreign to their upbringing. Yet, she was not ashamed. She was finding new confidence in her erotogenic appeal.

And this was not all. Some days after practice she was following Cornbread back to his place where they mostly discussed the act and he pointed out ways which she could tease the crowd and still not get arrested. Here, the agent and his client, were becoming friendlier--she relying on him more, he touching her more, here on the hip, here on the side of the breast. One day he kissed her, his mouth lingering a moment, a tip of tongue touching her tongue.

She liked it.

"This new shirt is gonna wow em, darling," Cornbread was saying one rainy morning after practice as they relaxed on his threadbare couch. He held up a sparkly piece of clothing no bigger than a handkerchief.

"I like it," Lilith said, feeling the artificial material. She rubbed a hand across her chest. "Ooh, I'm all sweat. That was a workout today."

"I have a shower," Cornbread said, gesturing toward a back room where they had never gone.

"That would be heaven."

Lilith strolled into the bedroom and found a squalid mattress and some clothes strewn about. A small bathroom not much bigger than the shower stall itself was to the left.

Lilith set the water on hot and peeled off her sticky clothing. Once under the spray she immediately felt invigorated and refreshed. She let the steaming water--ah, blessed thermae-- run into her mouth and onto the back of her neck. She felt cleansed inside and out. She was a new woman.

She was an American entertainer.

When she stepped out of the moldy stall Cornbread stood in the doorway, rapt.

Her hands went to her chest and crotch.

"You are as lovely as a diamond flush," he said with a shimmer.

She hesitated maybe a moment. There was no morality in her decision--she was all ache--there was only a brief mental picture, a flicker across her screen like a video pentimento, of her husband's grinning face. Then it was gone.

Lilith took her hands away and walked to him. She put her mouth against his and her warm wet body pressed against his clothes, making an impression on the length of him, like a snow angel.

His hands slid all over her and she abandoned herself to the pleasure. It was like the appreciation of her audience. She was *good*.

He grasped her buttocks and pulled her hard against him and she felt his erection through his white pants and when she backed up to unbuckle him she could see through the now damp material the outline of his dark member meaning he was underwearless, either from design or he had none, and she soon had him out in the air and its girth surprised her, she ran her hand down its knotty length fingering the veins like she fingered her squeege, squeezing its round helmet while Cornbread oofed and writhed, its dark size like the thick sausages she loved back home and she knelt and took it into her mouth and it swelled against her cheeks and she relished its warmth and tightness on her tongue.

Later when Cornbread entered her, on the dirty mattress, her sitting on him like a cowgirl, she thought she was not big enough but she was so wet he slid in with ease and pumped her full of his warm American sperm until she threw her head back, barking "Uckfay, oh My Cornbread, Uckfay me!"

All this while she polished her act, her audience grew, she knew a small fame in the Midsouth area, young folks coming from Pigott, Arkansas; Hernando, Mississippi; Kennett, Missouri; and points beyond. She soon had callow swains at her feet as she performed, looking at her with more than a musical appreciation. And accordingly she outgrew her venue and Lady Madeline was forced to open her curtained backroom, move the stage and put in a dozen more small tables. Business was good and the great woman began to bask in the reflected glow of Lilith's celebrity and, surprisingly to all, she began to shed pounds like a stripper casting aside veils. What was revealed underneath the layers of poundage was an equally unattractive, manly woman with large bosoms and a face all but invisible without stratums of pancake and paint.

And Seth grew inconsolable.

Soon he was not even attending performances but staying behind in the dingy Akimbo Arms, either drinking rotgut alone in his room, or worse, spending long wasted hours in the lobby listening to the malignant and fatuous verbosity of Mr. Grimus. It was a downward spiral to end all downward spirals, all the more terrible for the formerly jovial personality of its victim.

"Adamson," Mr. Grimus phlegmed. "You losing that woman of yours."

"Hccccgh," Seth nodded sadly.

"Pick youself up by the soiled seat a you pants and get that bitch back," Grimus offered, sagely.

"I dunno, Mr. Grimus."

"I know, boy. I seen it time and time again immermorial. I had the gals once, you bet. I know the drill."

And here Grimus laughed until he coughed up an army green something at his own unintended pun.

"Ha ha, Mr. Grimus. I'm too low to pick my sad self up. I'm reaching back for my own pants seat and finding only air, yes."

"Adamson, Adamson," the stickman said, bringing himself back from the edge of emphysema. "You gotta fight boy."

"I'm no fighter."

"I don' necessarily mean with you pitiful fisticuffs, ya dingy Pollock."

"I'm no fish, Mr. Grimus. I'm just a man sinking down."

"Look, Adamson. Just up the street here we gots conjure men put a spell on the offending parties, give you something get the lead back in you rifle, win the heart of your truly beloved back. Now it'll cost you, make no mistake. You slip me a sawbuck or two and I steer you right, count on it. Whaddya say?"

"I don't follow so well."

"Magic men, buddy. You got magic men back home, huh?"

"We have no magician back home, no. We have wonderful opera, you ever see--"

"Adamson, I'm trying to help you, son. Attend. You want me set you up with some of our local hoodoo, you just say the word."

Seth appeared to think this over but through his alcoholic shadows only an inkling of light leaked.

"I don't need magic, Mr. Grimus. I need putting down. I'm lost man. I'm ex-human."

"So be it. Now get away from the desk, outlander. You so sad you bad for business."

As Cornbread began to roll in Lilith's money not to say her arms his outlook on life began to go through a sea change. It was not so much that integrity could get a toehold as that Cornbread could afford a more generous attitude generally.

And Lilith, Americanized to a fault, affecting swinger outfits and hairstyle (hiphuggers on her macrocarpous proportions causing the bugs to be let loose in her manager/ lover), was, as one drunken patron or more attested, a "hot little number."

Cornbread moved them into a slightly more upscale apartment where their trysts took on a new vigor and after christening each room with their lovemaking (especially savoring the Formica countertop where Cornbread set Lilith's bare buttocks while he stooped uncomfortably and supped like a communicant while the graceful woman squealed and encouraged him in broken English) they would watch tv for hours between rehearsals, Lilith particularly falling for game shows and their gaudy delirium.

And the more tv and radio she absorbed the more she fell in love with her new home and its pop culture. She begged Cornbread to let her incorporate some of her new leanings into her act, most of all she wanted to sing a song she had heard, entitled "I Am Woman, Hear Me Roar." Cornbread remained adamant.

"We ain't doing that honky radio shit, honey. Memphis is a soul and blues town. We'll stick to what got us where we are, ok?"

"Aw, Cornbread. I'm tired of the blues. I don't have no blues, I'm happy woman."

"Yeah, well too happy can ruin a career, believe me. People don't identify with too happy."

"You no want me happy?" she simpered, smiling a little kitten smile and crawling toward him on their spacious new davenport.

"I want you happy here and I want you with the blues, pro-fessionally. You dig?"

"I dig," she said, smiling broadly as she took his dangly, but still surprisingly thick, member into her fingers.

"Posture, posture," she whispered, lowering her mouth toward what had become an addiction for her, this generous American penis, as dark as Beale, as dark as the spot on her soul.

One morning Seth awoke stinking of stale fermentation and his wife was not there and he didn't care and as the fog cleared he found a new anger at not caring.

"Lilith," he spoke aloud. "Up with this I will not put." He whispered it to the shadows in the corner, to the spider in his high-flung web. And outside, in the bedraggled courtyard of the Arms, a mockingbird sang as if in response.

Seth showered down the hall and put on a semi-clean suit and went out into the sunshine. Its brightness almost caused him to retreat, so long had it been since he had ventured out of doors, daytime. He squinted like Mr. Magoo toward Beale. His feet began shuffling that way.

Once on Beale he looked east and he looked west and he knew not what to do. From the river came the early morning sounds of movement, barges perhaps, or steamboats. Men working. Folks setting out on travels. Mark Twain. And, from somewhere closer, the smell of frying onions hit Seth like a tonic and he shook his webby head and opened his peepers a bit wider.

He wandered. He bumped into empty doorways, repeating the perambulations he and Lilith undertook on their first day on the fabled thoroughfare. Lilith. He had to stop and steady himself against a derelict parking meter.

He found himself at the entrance to Schwab's Dry Goods before he realized he had moved. He was dazed by the displays in the broad glass windows, items surely selected in the previous century and never thought of again. He went through the open door and found himself in the Emerald City of drugstores, the high ceilings, the wooden floors, the display bins full of drab, old-fashioned merchandise, the walls seemingly tilting left and right like some old expressionist movie set. It gave him vertigo just to stand there; he felt as if the commodities were crowding him about, hustling him from bin to bin. He was in some kind of funhouse, moving along a cockeyed consumer conveyor belt which bumped him here and there. Also, there seemed to be no other human presence.

Seth lighted in one corner of the store, his head swimming, his senses alive and tingling. As his focus sharpened he was standing in front of a wall of necromantic paraphernalia, a witch's panoply. He felt something in his hand and it was a small vial, decorated with a poorly rendered female figure and, in crude red lettering, the legend Love Potion. His heart raced.

He roamed the emporium, clutching the vial in his sweaty palm. Upstairs he found a makeshift museum and he absentmindedly read the histories before him. Beale Street seemed pickled here, reduced to its purest, hardened core by time and disinterest, an antediluvian saga. Seth felt as if the street was talking to him and he found a power within himself. For the moment, anyway, he did not want a drink.

At the end of one counter, cobwebbed and dusty, almost obscured by tarnish he espied a glass bottle, of the type normally full of cider or moonshine. And, through the webs time had woven he thought he saw movement, a buglike flitting within the glass.

Seth picked it up and wiped his sleeve across the dimmed surface. There was a small, dingy label, with a faded blue ink notation: *homo lupus homini.* Inside was a small animal, manlike on two stick-y legs, hairy like an emaciated rat, and it was gesturing wildly at Seth, slapping the glass with one tiny paw and holding his ruby-tipped penis with the other. A masturbatory demon bent on escaping, Seth figured. Well, he would be no party to it and set the diabolical jug back where he had found it, even obscuring it more with some old washcloths and superannuated papers lying about.

Once back in the privacy of his lodging Seth read the instructions on the paper label of his container of love potion. He was to twine together one of his hairs with one of Lilith's and burn them in a small pyre along with a pinch of the pinkish powder in the vial and there were some sample phrases to chant, only as suggestions, the final spell by necessity having to come from the user's own heart. Seth felt up to it.

Finding one of Lilith's lovely chestnut hairs was easy enough and plucking one of his own he twined them together as best he could. They seemed to not want to join and after twisting them strenuously they would unwind the instant he removed his hand. Finally he managed with a little spittle to make them into a semblance of oneness and he lay them across the diminutive mound of powder he had sifted into a cheap ashtray. When he placed the flaming match to the concoction the spit prevented it from catching right away. It smoldered and smoked a bit, the powder producing a stink like frizzling fruit. A small scarlet genie of smoke rose into the room and the hairs sizzled and that was it; the spell was cast. He forgot to say a word but he was satisfied with the drama of his puny fizgig. Seth lay back on the bed and thought about a quick poteen but decided against it and soon he was sleeping the sleep of the dreamless warrior.

That night Seth showed up at Rix, cleaned up and smiling, and when he entered Cornbread did not at first recognize him. Seth strolled over and shook the big man's thick-fingered hand.

"Good evening, Mr. Slunt. Good crowd tonight."

"Yas," Cornbread said, recovering with the recognition of the funny foreigner. "Seth, it's good to have you back, man."

"Lilith about to commence?" Seth's speech seemed oddly clipped as if he were making a concerted effort to speak in a refined manner.

"Sit down, sit down. Right up front here, best seat in the house."

When the lights went down and Lilith sauntered out onto the stage in her skimpy costume, her perfect round bosoms pushed into mounds of confection by the latticework underneath them, her eyes latched onto her husband right away and she smiled a warm smile, as personal a salutation as Seth had seen in many a silvery moon.

The songs that Lilith belted out that night, in her rusty door hinge of a voice, tore through Seth like a surgery. When she whined "Cowbell Blues," when she ripped up "Cadwallader Jones and the Widow Woman," when she bumped through "Spotlight on your Mister," Seth wept like a child. It was during the latter number, with its suggestive chorus, that Lilith was writhing like a tent-show dancer, her hands pushing her pushed up breasts out of their encasements, her hands running down her bedecked costuming. And, here, at one hot point, singing

> Lowdown on me baby
>
> Go lowdown
>
> Unneltay into me sugar
>
> Go on down

Lilith's eyes opened, burning red like a creature of legend, and pierced her husband's gentle, blue gaze. Seth felt pincers in his chest like an incubus there, and lower down, his member stirred for the first time in weeks, and unashamed he let it post there, like a lighthouse, like a beacon for his wayward wife.

That night Lilith went straight home with Seth and fell asleep sweetly against his shoulder, saying nothing, and Seth lay there all night, thinking he had won the battle, had conquered the forces of unrest so plentiful here in the land of the free and foolish.

In the morning when he awoke she was gone without a note.

Rehearsal that morning was a waste, a lost ship in the ocean of musical history. Outside a storm like *The Poseidon Adventure* raged relentlessly, small trickles making their way through the club's permeable roof, making more music in various pots and pans than the three musicians were managing on stage.

"Fuck it," the drummer said. Rising from behind his kit and throwing a smoky glance around the room, he ducked out into the tempest.

"Whatsay we call it a day? Sugar, let's take a retreat back to the digs and unwind, huh?" Cornbread said, touching Lilith on the bicep much like he did when they first met.

Lilith pouted like the face of tragedy and moving her from the club was like shifting about a bag of treelimbs.

Once under Cornbread's roof, wet and anxious, they fell onto the bed and Lilith sighed with a steamkettle's resign.

"Les get you out of those wet things," Cornbread said, undressing her and rubbing her wet, white body with a cheap towel. She looked like a corpse and her fixed visage was a corpse's and the man's tender kisses on nipple or hip were met with a corpse's indifference.

"You rest here, sugar," Cornbread said, giving up in the face of such azoic anaphrodisia, and exited quickly, a prisoner set free. He went out into the now waning rainfall and walked the streets where he was known, looking for that old knowledge, that solid ground.

Lilith lay where she was left and slept not. She was in a funk, no doubt. Her music didn't move her. Her husband was a drunk, or a recovering drunk or whatever he was. And her lover's thick, swart cock thrilled her not at all. This was cause for concern. She always wanted Cornbread--it was a steadying thing, her desire for him. She began to be frightened and her hospitable new country suddenly seemed vast and spooky. She was looking into the abyss and the abyss was tsking her like a Sunday school teacher. Last night she'd dreamed a horrific dream, all about being pursued by a monster, which would almost reach her and she would shimmy from his grasp. But he kept coming, on and on, as tireless as time, this wolfman with his hideous, wet mouth, almost reaching her, his paw, surprisingly warm, raking her naked shoulder--that's true, she was naked, outside, running, running and he was so close behind her, and then right before he wrapped his strong, hirsute arms around her from behind--she could feel his feverish breath on her skin--she woke up. Seth was sleeping beside her, grotesque in his childlike, wide-mouthed oblivion, a slight sonorous breathing coming from him.

She had dressed and run.

That night the club had to close because of water damage and Lilith was thankful for the night off. She looked at her husband who sat grinning at her from the armchair and she felt pity and very little love.

"What shall we do tonight?" Seth spoke, startling his wife. It was as if a puppet had suddenly sprung to life.

"Um, I don't know, husband. You want to make plans?"

"Yes, let's. A movie, perhaps."

This shocked the burnedout singer and she felt a flutter of excitement in her breast. She had never seen an American movie, so legendary back home.

"Oh, can we?" she said, like a schoolgirl.

"Yes, we can," he said, "let's."

The movie they saw baffled them no end. They could not keep up with the plot twists and the nonstop action was like tympani in their heads. It was very unsettling. They thought they had stepped unwelcome into an alternate universe and when they stepped back into the Memphis night they walked as if unsure the world was still aright. It further confused the already confused Lilith.

Seth spoke first.

"This motion picture, I do not know. I do not understand so well."

"Also I was blistered," Lilith said.

"What is blistered?"

But Lilith did not answer.

"This *200 Motels*, you think this is the way of all movies? They are too sophisticated for us I'm thinking," she said.

"I think I did not follow so good, but maybe just because I was by your side again."

Lilith looked at her husband and slipped her hand into his.

"Husband mine," she said. "I think we should stick to *Let's Make a Deal*," and before it was out of her mouth she realized she had never watched this show with Seth.

"What is this?"

"Nothing," she said and smiled at him.

Lilith came to bed that night without a nightdress, an unprecedented display. Seth's heart was a cudgel.

Without planning to Lilith reached over and ran her hand down the front of her husband's thin pajama bottoms. He sprang into her grasp. She tugged the loose elastic pants away and felt the cool, thin length of him. It had been a long time. Seth began to cry silently, as she worked him up and down.

Lilith sat up and looked at her husband and did not necessarily recognize him. When she put her mouth over him he was aware of a cunning new magic afoot. She had done this thing before but now it was with a religious abandon. And when he came into her cheeks he was replenished as if God had entered the room, reborn as husband and man, and Lilith, too, felt something stirring as she enveloped his center, a prickle of holiness, maybe, something light, bright and inchoate.

Day by day Seth and Lilith rediscovered each other, at first like young lovers whose only interest is that plumbable region underneath attire. Lilith's stage act became a focused and fiery expression, her previously misdirected sexual energies finding a home base in her appreciative suitor-husband. And, when the sex settled into comfortable routine, when it again became a lambent mediation on unloneliness, Seth and Lilith found each other as new relatives, allies in the fairytale world of the USA.

They were like forest creatures, awakened far from home with only their instincts and perceptions and each other as sensible tethers. And they became a twosome.

Cornbread, he just sort of wandered away, that first frost of frigidity from his lover enough to send his shallow heart into retreat. Oh, he made a perfunctory show of desire thwarted ("Honey, we good together" "Sugar, you ain't got no act without me.") but in the end he took a healthy severance pay and hit the streets running.

It's told he found a new act, a tall, chesty white woman with a voice like rhubarb pie, who sang top 40 standards and played Holiday Inn lounges with her long-haired combo. She had a minor radio hit with "You're Standing On My Train." And he had a career of sorts, in the peripatetic Memphis music business, today a success, tomorrow friendless, the next day a rediscovered jewel. It was, as they say, the way it was.

Lilith's career took off, well, it was the late seventies and the next big thing was only as close as the next best thing and gimmicks abounded and lesser lights flared out briefly in the dim gloaming of pop desire and Lilith's voice was as curious as any act with foot-high pompadours. Her reliance on roots music gave way at least partwise to Reddy-made mass euphony and the shaky marriage of the two produced a sound unlike any heard before on these shores which have witnessed many an eccentricity. In short she was hot.

A man from Rounder Records (as opposed to square, Seth supposed) came round and expressed great interest in the foreign songbird and a deal was struck and a record was released. It was a new dawn.

And Seth found himself not an outsider anymore when he discovered deep inside an uncanny ability to pen blues material for his wife to shape in her own insidious manner into hit record material. Some of his songs remain standards today, if only in the decidedly marginal world of Memphis music. He wrote "Walk Away from Me Backwards." He wrote "Tumble Me Like a Rock." He wrote "Nanny Divine's Eternal Light." He wrote "Chloe Dark One Blues." He wrote "Standard Woke Up This Morning Blues," and "Sleepin on a Motorcycle." And, of course, his most famous lyric, the time-honored ditty with which his name is eternally linked, "Mississippi Lowdown Blues," with its irresistible

Now hows I sposed to feel

About somethin like that?

Seth and Lilith moved into a new apartment, a little nicer, more room, more ambience--they bid Mr. Grimus a not-so-fond adieu--and bought a bright new television and Lilith taught Seth the enchanted passageways of American sitcoms.

"This is a later episode, after Ellie the druggist absquatulated. That's Helen Crump. Cornbread says she's Boss Crump's daughter."

"Who's Boss Crump?" Seth ignored the reference to the impish ex-manager.

"I'm not sure. I think he played Beale in the old days."

Ah Beale, Beloved Beale, Street of Dream and Mirage: the newly affluent couple still couldn't stay away. They wandered its ghostly sidewalks, stopping occasionally in front of a lone street musician who plucked desultorily on a beatup guitar. There were always musicians outside, even in those days as if they were the city's memory, or maybe, the clarion, the carrion, the carried over, or the small bit of magic left over with which the future sows its heartening seeds. The foreigners never tired of the boulevard's shabby cheeriness: from it they drew their sustenance; from it Lilith comprehended the heart of this big foolhardy country.

One day there was a sign taped onto a dusty glass door on the south side of the street. Lilith saw it from across the park and was drawn to it with stately curiosity. She read it from between the strands of her hair blowing over her prominent brow: New Club Opening Soon. And she walked away happy.

And her happiness was almost a physical feeling, a fluttering down deep. Yet she was not aware, not yet, of the small tangibility beginning in her, the tumbling zygote, the color of chocolate milk, free floating, looking for a place in her to attach itself, with its tentative message of replenishment.

Epilogue

The Night Elvis Came to Beale Street:
A Children's Story

Listen, Children:

And so we went down to the Club BingoBango on Beale—and this was in O 1950something when Beale was still Beale I think you know what I mean. And there were four of us, near as I can recollect, Henry the Hammer Jensen and Styx Ygg, the drummer for the BamBam Five, Sweet Annie Divine and myself.

There was news out on the street and the Club was the center of that news and well we were just as likely to be involved as not.

Henry and Styx were gigging at the club, playing their own short-attention-span versions of the blues, and the lead singer, when it wasn't Sweet Annie Divine, was a cat named Sammy Peeps, from Moosejaw, Mississippi, who sang like a dog with a star for a brain. He sang real good.

Now the blues was the music and the music made Beale and the men who made the music were treated like the royalty they wanted to be treated like and the music flowed

like religion and many men and women were made less blue
by the blues. It was in the air.

Though Beale was dying, I have to be honest, its best
days done past, and sometimes I think the only glue which
held poor Beale Street upright in these godly days was the
blues, yes it was. Styx thought so too and did his best to keep
it up, often playing twentyfour hours straight with no breaks
and very little sustenance. He may have been held upright by
the blues hisself.

And on this steamy night I'm discussing the four
of us were standing on the sidewalk outside the Club and
tanning under the lights of the heart of the city and watching
constellations wheel and scatter taking a break themselves
just as the musicians were. This was Memphis, Tennessee in
the days after the War and we were a fairly happy people all in
all.

Annie looked down Beale and scrunched up her face
and said in her drippy Arkansas drawl,

"Lord, it's hot tonight and it's always hotter on Beale I
believe."

Well, the rest of us could only nod and mutter.

Something caught our attention and I don't rightly
know why but looking back at the wonder of it I think it was
the sudden silence. We all looked up toward Lansky's and on
the sidewalk outside of Lansky's stood this skinny white kid
with gassed back hair and a lean and hungry look and eyes
as big as the moon and he was looking back at us. It was a
transfixing moment and I don't have to explain why.

And he started sauntering our way.

Styx, who was nervous at the best of times, attuned
into something distant he was, grew all over calm.

Under his breath he said, "Here comes history, people."

And we all looked at him and then back at the kid coming toward us, closer now.

The kid, head down like a tracking hounddog, stood at the curb and shuffled his loafered feet like he was collecting his young thoughts and we were held in suspension like he was gonna ask us for our lifeblood and we were obliged to give it to him, don't you see.

The kid looked up and there was spirit in his river-brown eyes and he sort of mumbled but we were speaking his language and glommed on right away and he said,

"Do you think if I can't read music it'll hold me back?"

And the mood was reverential and the neon started to hum again and around the world, where the Sun was, there was a new dawn aborning but here on Beale the five of us were wide awake in a night full of promise and we fell together and returned to the blessed cave of BingoBango.

Now this kid says his name is Elvis and we all said yes I guess it is and we surreptitiously pulled our Bibles out and tried to find the place where that name came from and we didn't, you know. And I think Elvis kind of fell in love with Annie Divine, because what man didn't, and she was sweet to him because Sweet she was, and when Annie got up to sing Elvis was starstruck you could see.

And the night went on and it got later and later (or earlier, if you like, being the morning hours were here and accountable) and the music flowed around us and the new kid just sat there soaking it up.

Sitx was flamming like a pent-up horse and that lonesome guitar was pouring out some liquid animation and Sammy Peeps was bellowing with all his heart which was the only way we ever heard Sammy sing.

And Elvis said,

"Man sounds like Big Boy Crudup."

And we said yes, and suddenly Styx was pulling the kid up onto the stage with the band and the kid was looking at his feet and the band was laying down some lowdown bottom and then Elvis he just let the angels take him and he launched into some gospel phrasings and was singing from some deep place and we all nodded yes and we understood something together, something new.

Elvis sang:

Mama told me yeah

Woke up this morning

Lonely yeah for someone

Mama done told me

And even Willy the bartender who was somber as a coyote was seen bobbing his head and smiling a little at this new thing, at this kid from Twobelow, this Elvis.

Well, a good time was had by all, yes, and after hours, sometime in the new day, the five of us, and a sixth, Red Rolly Kastlecream, baseball's first black shortstop I think he was, strode out of the Club onto the sidewalk and perambulated down westward talking and cutting up and patting this kid on the back. And he was laughing and happy as all get out you could see and we moved on.

Down past the Blue Light, past Lansky's, down past the café where they were already frying up the catfish for the next day I believe, and we ended up on the bluff overlooking the river and we sat down tired and delighted and a quietness settled over us.

Elvis,

we all said,

you coming back to Beale soon.

And he was tickled and got Dewey eyed as the first salmon-colored rays of dawn appeared over the sluggish waters of the Mississippi. And Annie, the Duchess of Beale Street, leaned over and kissed the kid on the cheek and this was seen as a blessing you might say, a simple and subtle coronation. She was passing a little of disappearing but eternal Beale on.

And Elvis just sat there looking into Arkansas and beyond and into the tumbling thoughtful water as if he could see the future there and I guess he could, children.

We all thought, yes, maybe he could.

COREY MESLER lives to write and writes to live. He has been called—but never to his face—a prophet. If he has seen farther than other men it is because he has stepped on the shoulders of anyone who gets in his way. All of his publishing credits he dedicates to his wife and two children, with the exception of the poem "Lungfish Melody," which he wrote out of a self-destructive desire to meet the actress Heather Graham.

www.ingramcontent.com/pod-product-compliance
Lightning Source LLC
Chambersburg PA
CBHW050323110726
47899CB00007B/2343